REAGANISTA

Heaven's Blueprints for
America's Return to Glory

Annie Blouin,
MBA

ISBN 978-1-63814-910-1 (Paperback)
ISBN 978-1-63814-911-8 (Digital)

All scripture that is referenced was taken
from the NKJV.

Covenant Books
11661 Hwy 707
Murrells Inlet, SC 29576
www.covenantbooks.com

To my son, Joseph Daniel Blouin

To whom much is given, much is required.
— Luke 12:48

Preface

A Republic, if you can keep it.
— Benjamin Franklin

I wrote *Reaganista* in the spring of 2020, in the beginnings of what would be over a year-long season that tried men's souls in America and the world. I didn't anticipate the trauma our great nation would endure in coming out from the death grip of truly evil cabal elitists. Our fight for freedom, not only for our nation but for the world, was imperative for the survival of so many. Freedom. Freedom. Oh the precious reality of freedom.

Acknowledgments

✦

Thanks to Jesus for His love and His truth, for always and forever.

Thank you to all my dear intercessor friends who prayed this book into existence. I couldn't have done this without all of you. You'll be richly rewarded in heaven for your service to the King and His kingdom.

Special thanks to Claudia.

Thanks to my dear husband, Joe.

Thanks to Jennifer Sanders for the beautiful cover art design. http://www.iseeallofyou.com

Thanks to Covenant Books and all the wonderful people on the team.

Thanks to President Donald J. Trump, our beautiful First Lady Melania, their family, our military intelligence insider, and our valiant military.

Chapter 1

❧❧❧

"**G**ood morning, Kay, Ann, and Daniel." Ava hugged her children and kissed them on the top of their tousled heads.

Kay and Daniel quickly busied themselves getting ready for school, but Ann clung to her mom.

"What's wrong, honey?" Ava asked, lifting Ann's head to look in her eyes.

"I had a bad dream," Ann said, looking frightened.

"Do you want to tell me about it?" Ava asked her young daughter as she pulled her into her arms and sat at the kitchen table with her.

"Okay, Mommy. I dreamed we were driving in San Francisco, and all of a sudden, the ground started shaking. Buildings started falling down, and the highway split open, and cars fell through. People were running and screaming. It felt so real, and I was so scared."

"I'm sorry, Ann, you are safe. You don't need to be afraid."

"I was so sad for the people."

"What do you think we should do?" Ava asked Ann.

"Pray?"

"Right. Jesus never blessed storms. He commanded them to stop. So we too can command the earthquake not to happen like Jesus would have done," Ava said.

"Can we do that?"

"Yes, honey. Jesus gave us the keys to the world when He went to heaven, remember?" Ava asked. "Jesus gave us, as His body, authority over the world to keep people safe and make earth like heaven. He gave us authority over the weather and the earth."

Slowly, her little face was relaxing as she felt God's solution unfolding.

Another question occurred to Ann, "Why does the earth shake?"

"Underneath the earth's surface, pressure builds up and then releases through fault lines which are like cracks. Remember at the lake when we saw that child shake a soda can? What happened when his brother opened it?"

"It sprayed everywhere!" Ann giggled.

"The earth can get like that soda can too and needs to release the pressure. Do you think that God is judging people with earthquakes, hurricanes, and tornadoes?" Ava asked her daughter.

"No, Mommy. Why would God do that? He loves us."

"You're right, Ann. God isn't judging or punishing for sin now. When you asked Jesus to forgive you for your sins, God forgave you. When you get to heaven because your sins were forgiven through Jesus, God will judge your life by rewarding you for the good you do and how you stewarded your life. For people who didn't choose Jesus's forgiveness while they were alive, they will be judged for their sins and will be forever separated from God."

"That's so sad. I think that makes Jesus's heart hurt. I've seen Him crying for the people who don't know Him."

Ava was so touched by her daughter's tender heart of love for people.

"God's heart is full of love and compassion. The Bible says that the kindness of God leads to repentance. I don't understand why people would think that God sends earthquakes or disasters to judge people for their sins."

"Why do they think that?" Ann asked.

"Because they don't know how good He is. He's only good. There is no darkness in Him. God set up spiritual laws in the world like gravity in the natural world; only, these laws exist in the unseen world. For example, the principle of sowing and reaping is a spiritual law in effect in the world. Whatever a person plants, they will receive a harvest in that. What do you get when you plant an apple seed?"

"An apple tree."

"Can you get a lemon tree from the apple seed?"

"No! That would be silly!" Ann laughed, imagining the thought.

"It's the same with good things or bad things. When we plant seeds of kindness and love, we grow good relationships. When people plant seeds of bitterness or gossip or hatred, they reap a harvest of destructive relationships. That's not God judging us; that is just the fruit of our own choices. He advises us to choose wisely so that we have good harvests and good lives."

Kay and Daniel were listening as they ate their breakfast.

Kay joined the discussion by saying, "I've heard people say that some cities, like San Francisco, have a lot of sin, and others say God will judge the city for their sin, and that's what earthquakes are."

"It is true that there are cities where there is a lot of sin. Las Vegas is even nicknamed "Sin City." The principles of sowing and reaping exist, and there are certainly harvests or consequences to sin. But God's heart is conveyed in the Bible where He says, 'Where sin abounds, grace abounds much more'. God's heart is to bring His kindness, His love, and His forgiveness to bring healing to the people," Ava explained.

"How does He bring His love to cities and the people there?" Daniel asked insightfully.

"He does that through His children. When we extend God's mercy instead of judging for the sin we see, the Lord releases His kindness. Mercy always triumphs over judgment," Ava said.

"Wow, heavy conversation for an early morning!" Ava's husband Joe said as he walked into the kitchen. He leaned over and kissed his wife and daughter.

"I had a bad dream, Daddy, about an earthquake."

"I'm sorry, Ann. Are we going to pray?"

"In a minute. We were talking about God's perspective first so we know how to pray to release His goodness," Ava said. "The Bible tells us that the earth groans under the weight of sin, and creation groans for the sons of man to rise up into who they are. Who can explain what that means?"

"I think I know," Kay said.

She is the oldest of the three Wellington children. She is a petite young teenager with acting, singing, and dancing aspirations.

Her dramatic personality keeps the family laughing.

"The land of San Francisco feels the burden that the sin there carries and starts to collapse under the weight. If God's children don't know who they are, walk in their identity in Christ, and the power and authority that God gave us, the land, the city, and the people suffer. We're supposed to release God's forgiveness, His mercy, and His power through signs and wonders. When we do that, the earth is released from the weight of sin, and the atmosphere changes where people can discover the love Jesus has for them."

"That's exactly right, Kay. I'm so proud of you. Daddy and I are so thankful that you know who God is and who you are in Him."

"I'm not afraid anymore, Mommy. Can we pray now?" Ann asked.

"Sure. Do you want to start?"

"I bless San Francisco. God, I ask for Your forgiveness for the sin that is there. I ask for Your mercy, Your love, Your goodness, and Your healing power to permeate the entire Bay Area. Please keep people safe on the playgrounds there. Give them dreams and visions and encounters with You," Ann concluded.

"God, I say no to a large destructive earthquake in San Francisco. I pray that the earth would slowly and gently release the pressure that is built up and that there would be no damage and that nobody would be hurt," Kay said.

Daniel chimed in, "I saw a rainbow of God's promises over the city. I agree with You, God, that all of Your promises for the people of San Francisco would happen, that people would know Your love, and that Christians in the city would bring Your healing and miracles and that words of life would be spoken over the people and the area. I pray that people would turn from sin and come to know You, Jesus."

"That's great. Ann, ask God if we need to pray any further for the earthquake not to happen," Ava instructed her pretty preteen daughter. Ann carried the grace and love and mercy of God's heart. Even at a young age, she was an intercessor to bring God's will to situations. God often spoke to her in dreams to have her pray to change the course of history.

Ann closed her eyes while she listened to God and then she spoke. "He said we stopped it. It will release gradually and not noticeably now."

"Great! Good job, world changers! You need to get ready for school now, but first ask God for one thing He wants you to declare to bless the Bay Area," Joe instructed his family.

He was constantly amazed by his children's ability to hear from the Lord and how they naturally lived supernatural lives. They were growing up in a culture where their individual relationship with the Lord was paramount and was expressed through blessing others. Daniel, the youngest child, was an exceptional soccer player, had a brilliant mind, and a love for politics. Even at eleven years old, he understood the function of government and God's desire for the US. He listened raptly to his parents' detailed political discussions.

Daniel began the declarations. "The people of the Bay Area bring the beauty and creativity of Heaven to earth."

"I'm next," Kay said. "I declare San Francisco is a leader in financial responsibility in the US."

"I release God's protection to the Bay Area people in all areas of spirit, soul, and body," Ann declared.

"Another good day in the kingdom." Ava sighed with pleasure.

Chapter 2

⇒◇⇐

The Wellington family had lived in Northern California for seven years. They enjoyed the outdoor activities the Pacific Northwest had to offer, especially hiking to see the beautiful mountain waterfalls. Joe owned several small businesses and did business consulting and investing to help innovative new start-up companies succeed. He had a real heart for the people of his city to prosper. His wife, Ava, loved caring for their children and their home. In addition, as an avid prayer warrior, she and her friends went on prayer assignments from God. Their specialty was bringing change to the political realm. They fancied themselves as spies for God in the spiritual realm that brought righteousness to the natural world.

In recent years, Ava began private consulting to political leaders. She and a few friends were flying to Washington, DC later that morning to consult with their friend, Senator

Julia Thompson. A couple of years before, they had helped Julia secure an appointment as US Senator from California. They enjoyed the God-given assignment, which began with a middle of the night angelic encounter for Ava.

Ava and Joe met Julia and her husband Robert when they first moved to Redding, California. The Thompsons are a dynamic couple. They fell in love while they were getting business degrees from Wheaton College. They spent eight years working with orphans as missionaries in Romania. While they were in Romania, they began their own family and had four children. Upon returning to the United States, they made their money through construction in the real estate boom as well as through owning other investments and companies.

Julia has written several books on training leaders and raising children to be leaders. They are passionate about developing character in their children. They accomplish that in a number of ways. In the summers, Julia gives the children a reading list that includes the classics in American literature as well as biographies of great statesmen like Winston Churchill and Margaret Thatcher. She is training her children to be great leaders.

Robert always has them helping with projects. A few years ago, Robert and their four preteen and teenage children built a log cabin in the Trinity Alps. Now they go there as a family to fish, hike, and relax. The children were amazed by the accomplishment and really grew in their confidence in the abilities God has graced them with.

Julia is passionate about leadership. She was a member of the local school board, on the board of a large local corporation, and mayor of Redding. She is petite and known to be a classy, elegant dresser. Julia is also a classical pianist. She has taught all of her children to play as well. She mostly plays for relaxation and worship.

Now, as a Senator, Julia is a member of the US Senate Committee on Appropriations and had asked Ava to meet with the committee to help define their overall budgetary priorities. Ava, with her master's in business administration degree and her extensive study in political and fiscal policy, has substantial experience releasing the wisdom of heaven into political arenas.

This is an unprecedented time in the history of the nation. The United States as well as the entire world is reeling from the recent exposure of crime and evil. Some still refuse to believe it despite the overwhelming evidence and consequences. The arrests, imprisonments, and executions of tens of thousands of politicians on both sides of the aisle, celebrities, business executives, and the world elites for crimes of treason, sedition, money laundering, insider trading, human trafficking, pedophilia, and horrific satanic murder and sexual abuse of children have turned the world upside down. The recent biological, financial, electoral, and cyberattacks from China that nearly started a worldwide nuclear holocaust and the subsequent removal of the central banking system and the return of financial autonomy to the US treasury has stunned even the average citizen.

The sudden shifts and the worldwide financial and leadership ramifications have been staggering, to say the least. The president of the United States, along with the American people, is clamoring for major change and a return to the foundation the founding fathers wisely established. The budget and direction of the United States is in a crucial time in history. Without major changes, the US is in a free fall toward destruction. The political parties are in gridlock. The few remaining sitting senators and congresspeople who survived the massive purge of nationwide arrests know they're likely to be voted out of office in the next election if they don't establish radical, positive change. The old guard is changing, and only those on board with the apparent new direction will remain. With this awareness, the senators are desperately trying to form a coalition and direction.

The United States as well as the world is watching with baited breath as the government regroups. It is with this understanding of the kairos moment in time that Julia asked Ava to come into a private meeting to define the identity and purpose of the United States in a way that would enable the senators to have clear priorities for the United States' budget.

Chapter 3

❦

J oe and Ava kissed the children goodbye as they dropped them off at school and then went to walk the Sacramento River Trail together. They enjoyed the exercise, the scenery, and the time together. Ava, always the competitive one, looked for opportunities to race other walkers.

"Ava, you're like a racehorse!" Joe laughed as he saw her set her sights on the couple ahead of them and felt her increase the pace to pass them. Joe loved his spunky wife. A few days a week they enjoyed playing racquetball together. She was very good at judging the best angles to score winning shots and wasn't deterred by his superior strength. Joe, however, had the uncanny ability to hit the front wall so low that the ball literally rolled back along the highly polished floor, a completely indefensible shot. Ava declared those shots illegal when they played together. She would get mad, and he would only laugh harder. In their seventeen happy years of marriage, Joe always greeted Ava with a kiss hello and a kiss goodbye. They were very blessed to live the dream marriage. Like all couples, they had their disagreements, but they had a core value of honoring one another. Therefore, they treated one another with love and respect. Their first argument while they were dating was when Ava angrily shouted at Joe. He very calmly asked her what she was doing. Momentarily stunned into silence, she replied that they were fighting. He matter-of-factly told her, "Not like that, we're not." He proceeded to tell his feisty wife-to-be, "This is not a personal vendetta. I love you with all of my heart, and I will never intentionally hurt you. I promise to always treat you with honor and respect, especially when we disagree." At those words, Ava's anger melted, and through relationship with the man she knew loved her and would lay down his life for her, she learned to communicate honestly with respect for her man. That laid the foundation for a healthy marriage. Years later, they still preferred each other's company to anyone else's.

Spring had already come to Northern California. In late April, afternoon temperatures were well into the 80s. The winter rains had concluded; the rivers and lakes were full, and the air sparkled with the promise of new life. Joe and Ava finished their morning walk and returned home for Ava to shower and finish preparing for her trip. As Ava zipped her suitcase shut, her phone rang. It was Anna.

Anna was a spiritual mom to Ava and many others. She was a strong intercessor, moved powerfully in the prophetic, and loved to garden. She and her husband lived in their custom-built home in the eastern foothills of the Trinity Alps. She provided oversight for Ava and her team on their intercessory journeys.

"Hi, Anna. I'm glad you called."

"Hi, Ava. Are you getting ready to go?"

"Yes, I am nearly ready. I am picking up Jenna, Elle, and Alexa in an hour and then going to the airport."

Jenna, Elle, and Alexa and their husbands were good friends of Ava and Joe. The women had traveled together extensively on prayer journeys.

They all had children in elementary school and junior high and got together for play dates. Their friendships had developed as they partnered together in prayer. Ava reflected on how unique each of her friends were.

Elle and Charles Clark have three sons. Charles is a math teacher, very logical and analytical while Elle is creative and artistic. She is a children's book author. She wrote a series of adventure books for children where they travel to different nations and discover treasure in the people and cultures of the world. Through Elle's books, children all over the world learn how much their Father God loves them and has designed amazing destinies for their lives. Her own children are very sensitive to calling out destiny in other children. Elle and Charles have been told by the Lord that they are raising an "eagle's nest." The Lord gave them three sons, all very different, yet all called to be prophets for the body of Christ. Ava loved going to Elle's house. Elle is so creative; she loves variety and frequently paints her front door a different color. She also enjoys cooking and raises an herb and vegetable garden.

Ava met Jenna Hunter at a parenting class. Their sons were friends in preschool when the moms realized they knew each other too. Jenna met her husband Brian when they were both teaching junior high students. They taught their own children to read at a very young age. Jenna and Brian have a passion for activating the 90 percent of the brain that scientists say humans don't use. Jenna uses music therapy to develop the brain. She believes that as people learn from the Tree of Life rather than from the tree of knowledge that the mind of Christ will be established in God's children. She believes that the Spirit of wisdom and revelation that Scripture refers to will be used to disciple nations. Jenna also has an anointing to hear what the Lord is bringing the body of Christ at the beginning of each new year. For the past three years, Jenna's word for the year has coincided with the prophets of the land.

Alexa and Andrew Walker are a dynamic young couple. Andrew made his money in online trading and currently invests in small businesses to help young entrepreneurs get established. Alexa cares for their three sons and leads worship in church. She has recorded two worship CDs that bring the Lord's presence and glory in a fresh way. Alexa is an avid walker. She and Ava do prayer walks in their city together frequently. They both receive revelatory dreams from the Lord and enjoy interpreting them at a coffee shop while drinking iced chai lattes. They also like shopping and going to the spa together. Ava enjoyed her life and traveling about the world on her Father's business.

She listened as Anna continued, "Before you leave, I want to tell you that my team is covering all of you and your families in prayer. If the Lord shows us anything specific, I will let you know. We live in a different world than we even imagined. After everything that has been exposed recently in many world and Hollywood leaders financially, sexually, satanically, and treasonously, we need fresh vision for our world going forward. The exposure of the great world of iniquity of the deep state and other world leaders nearly brought our great nation to her knees. True repentance and a solid foundation in God will bring forth the destiny of our nation. Like we talked before, go share the identity and destiny of the United States with the senators. This will help them appropriate funds accordingly."

"Thanks so much, Anna."

"This is not business as usual. I know in your previous Washington, DC, meetings it was hit or miss for them to receive the wisdom of heaven. God has assured me, however, that they are all so shocked by recent world events and the arrests of many colleagues that they will hear and respond to what you have to say. Also, God told me He has a surprise for you on this trip. He will be giving you a desire of your heart."

"A desire of my heart? That sounds big and exciting! Do you know what it is?" Ava inquired.

"No, I just know that it is big, and you will be surprised."

Ava smiled broadly. Her primary love language was gifts. She loved to give and receive gifts, and she loved the anticipation of receiving a gift from God.

"I am even more excited for this trip now!" Ava exclaimed. "I bought a couple pieces of prophetic jewelry from Kingdom

Creations for Julia and Lauren. Both necklaces come with a prophetic word. I picked out the jewelry I was drawn to for each of them and then read the word. Both are perfect."

"They will love that! I didn't know you were going to see Lauren too."

"Yes, she'll take the Metro to DC for dinner with us and join us in our meetings."

"Wonderful! I wonder if anything funny will happen in this trip with Lauren?" Anna asked.

"I sure hope so!" Ava and Anna both laughed.

Lauren was a beautiful intercessor—a friend of Julia's who lived outside of Washington, DC; to help with Julia's appointment strategy to the US Senate a couple years ago, Lauren volunteered to do any prophetic acts in DC while Ava and her team prayed in California. It was a great cross-country joint effort. While doing so, Lauren was mistaken for a Hollywood actress and was chased by the paparazzi through the halls of the National Museum of Natural History and had to be driven secretly to the US Capitol Building by museum security. She barely made it on time and sheepishly told her tale to Ava. Two years later, everyone still laughed at her adventure. Julia's husband, Robert, particularly enjoyed laughing at their friend's expense. For undercover prayer assignments, Lauren normally camouflaged her strikingly good looks so that she didn't attract undue attention.

"Thanks for praying for us Anna. We couldn't do this without all of you. Your prayer covering and the church's spiritual covering protects all of us and clears the spiritual air-waves for us to accomplish God's purposes."

"You're very welcome. As you know, years ago, God showed us that as we focus on Him and release what He is saying and doing, we displace the enemy by bringing God's kingdom. When God's kingdom takes space that was previously occupied by demonic forces, no vacuum is left to be filled and king-dom building occurs. We also discovered that when we partnered intercessors in our healing rooms alongside the healing teams, instantly, the number of miracles we saw each week doubled. As the intercessors worshipped and brought God's presence, the resistance from the enemy greatly decreased. By connecting with God, the intercessors ruled the airwaves, and the angelic defeated the demonic, which allowed the healing to come into the physical realm."

Ava said, "I think intercessors by nature are warriors. Their spirits are strong and they love a good fight."

"You're right. Intercessors are warriors in the spirit in the same way that elite military forces are in the natural realm. When intercessors don't understand their role in fueling the angelic to fight and can't sense their effect in the spiritual realm, their warrior nature can be dissolved into focusing on the enemy. I pray God would show them their impact, and their warrior nature would be fulfilled by rescuing people and bringing God's solutions to problems, that and as they plunder the enemy's camp by bringing healing and restoration to people where there was once destruction and chaos, they will be satisfied." Anna said.

"Thanks for the reminders and for sharing your experience and wisdom with me. I know that learning from you saves me years of painful lessons," Ava said.

"That's the point of inheritance. Each generation is enabled to run farther and faster because of it."

"I appreciate it. I will keep you posted about our journey and let you know of any prayer requests. Thanks again. Love you."

The women hung up.

Ava checked the time, turned to Joe and said, "Thanks for loading the car and for taking the morning off to be with me. I have a little more time. Do you want to go to From the Hearth for a late breakfast?"

"Sure."

They often went to the cozy café for a specialty coffee or a meal.

When they were seated eating veggie omelets and whole grain toast, Ava cradled her mocha in the mug and declared, "I love mochas! Coffee, chocolate, and whipped cream, what could be better?"

Joe laughed. "Ava, you are such a study in contrasts. This morning, you drank an organic green smoothie of fresh vegetables and fruit for nutrition and now an omelet and a mocha."

"I'm pretty sure mochas and chocolate are in heaven too." Ava teased. "Seriously, though, one of the things after the shock of all that has been exposed in our true world history in banking, government, Hollywood, business, and the media, I want to help our government leaders with operating in discernment so that evil never gets a foothold in our nation again. I feel like I need to talk to the senators and staff about discerning of spirits and feeling in the spiritual realm. I know it will help a lot of people and give a much-needed framework to some people. I'm just not quite sure how to explain it. Any thoughts?"

Joe carried a big picture vision that Ava relied on.

"Start with the overview of what discernment/feeling is and then break it into smaller pieces. Your teaching gift will help them understand. Just wait on the Lord for when to share and whom to share with," Joe advised as they left the café and headed home.

"That's good. I realize it is the when to share and with whom that I am unsure about. You're right, God will show me."

Ava was primarily a feeler in the spirit. She had always discerned or sensed things in the spiritual realm like the Apostle Paul describes in 1 Corinthians 12:10: "And to another the gift to discern what the Spirit is speaking." She could feel, often through her spiritual emotions, what God was doing, what the demonic was doing, and what people's spirits were doing. She could sense the spiritual activity in individual people's lives, in businesses, in neighborhoods, in cities, in states, and regions. As her gifting developed, she also frequently began to read people's thoughts. Before she knew God, she thought she was going crazy. She would walk into a store or a home and have a flood of emotions — sometimes positive and sometimes negative or a combination of both. She would experience major mood swings and was exhausted by the deluge of thoughts and emotions. She could drive into a city and feel what the people struggled with that were demonic strongholds and oppressions. She could also feel God's desire and plan and hope for the people in any given city or region. One day, God showed her that she was "feeling" or "sensing" what was in the spiritual atmosphere around her, and it wasn't her own reality. That key revelation set her free. The Lord told her that she had used her discernment to protect herself as a little girl by determining what was safe and what wasn't. She discerned very strongly the evil associated with drug use and knew to never go down that path. Later, understanding came that drug use was an illegal access into the spiritual realm and that the demonic used the counterfeit reality to torment people. The real hunger was for mystical, spiritual encounters with God. People who were drawn to drug use were often people who were gifted to fly high with the Holy Spirit in experiencing His reality. Ava's gift of discernment protected her from evil, but because it wasn't initially connected to the Holy Spirit, it was also a source of torment for her. The enemy rode in on her discernment to produce fear and make her feel crazy. God told her to ask Him to connect her discernment to Holy Spirit and to only feel and see what He wanted her to be aware of and to close access to what the enemy was parading before her. Immediately, the world became a lot quieter and more peaceful for Ava. Experiencing this new freedom was life changing. She then prayed for her children to connect their discernment to Holy Spirit. They became more peaceful too.

God began to show Ava that being a "feeler" was a gift from Him; she just had to learn to use it in a mature fashion. The purpose of the feeler gift is to discern good and evil and pray to shift it for God's purposes. He helped her to not only "take every thought captive to the obedience of Christ" but also to "take every emotion captive." Over the years, she learned to discern when an emotion came from the atmosphere and when it was truly her own emotion. She learned to shift atmospheres by releasing God's presence. With Him, He brought peace and joy. Ava's daughter Ann had a finely tuned seer gift that she moved powerfully in.

One day, Ava felt demonic oppression in their home which was targeting Joe's business ventures. Joe was at his office working late while Ava and the children ate dinner together. Ava felt uneasy and, aware of the battle, had been praying.

At the table, Ann announced, "I just saw Daddy walk down the hall."

"Oh?" Ava asked, instantly alert. "Remember, Daddy's not home. What did you see?"

"I saw a tall man with dark hair in the hall."

Ava knew Ann had seen into the spiritual realm and was seeing with her eyes what Ava was feeling or discerning in her spirit.

"Ask God what it is that you saw," Ava instructed her daughter.

Ann inquired of the Lord, and she heard Him say it was a demon.

"Okay, ask the Lord what kind," Ava said.

Kay interjected saying, "God said it's a spirit of fear."

That feels right, Ava thought. "What do we do about it?" Ava asked her children.

"We pray," Kay, Ann, and Daniel chorused.

"Good. Ann, because you saw it, why don't you pray, please?"

"Okay, Mommy. I command the spirit of fear and any other demonic forces to leave our house and property. I plead the blood of Jesus around us, our home, and Daddy. Lord, thank you for protecting us and having your angels take care of us. Amen."

Ava immediately felt the atmosphere in the house shift. The fear and evil were gone, and peace returned. Ava thanked Ann for praying, and they then enjoyed their evening.

Ava knew the feeler and seer gifts partner together very powerfully. The children were still young but already moved strongly in their giftings. Discernment can be difficult to learn to operate in primarily because it is hard to calibrate and confirm. People who have this gift often don't receive feedback or training to fine-tune what they discern. Discernment is also very prone to being skewed by the person's own filter on how they see the world and any lies they believe about God or people and any wounding they have. Often, they see the world as they are, not as it actually is. Add in the other dimension of "feelers" experiencing major mood swings until their gifting matures; most discerners never develop their gifting in an accurate or healthy way. The enemy can see who carries this gift and tries hard to invalidate them or take them out because once it is connected to Holy Spirit and mature, feelers are very powerful warriors for God's kingdom. A mature discernment gift can sense the enemy's plans, connect with God to hear His plan and strategy and, by releasing God's plans through prayer and declaration, can negate the enemy's plans.

Joe's voice brought Ava back from her musings, saying, "I'll miss you."

"Thanks for taking care of the kids, the house, and working while I'm gone," Ava said to Joe.

"I'm glad to do it. I am so proud of you and what you and the team are doing for this nation." Joe grabbed Ava in a big hug and kissed her gently.

"I pray the Lord bless you and keep you and cause His face to shine on you and give you peace."

"Thanks, honey. I love you." Ava smiled as she got into her SUV.

"I love you too. Have a good trip. I'll call you." Joe closed the car door and waved as Ava drove away.

Chapter 4

A va picked up Elle, Alexa, and Jenna, and together they drove to the airport to catch their flight to Washington, DC.

"I'm excited about our trip! Seeing friends, eating, seeing the cherry blossom trees, eating, praying, eating, prophesying, eating..." Elle trailed off, laughing.

"Me too!" Jenna and Alexa chorused.

All four friends erupted into laughter. They were all thin and very fit and into exercising and health food, but true to form, they enjoyed the social prospect of eating together on their intercessory trips. They settled into their seats for the flight to the nation's capital. Ava encouraged each one to take some time to soak in the Lord's presence to stay connected to His heart and to get any further instructions or strategies from Him for their journey.

At the conclusion of the long flight, the women debarked from the plane, retrieved their bags, and took an Uber to their hotel. The drive through the city was beautiful. The cherry blossom trees were in full bloom and gave the city a pretty, decorative feel.

"My favorite time of the year to come to Washington, DC," Elle exclaimed.

With her artistic eye, she studied the trees to replicate in her next painting.

"I agree. I love the monuments at night. I've also been here over the Fourth of July and enjoyed the fireworks. I prefer the spring weather to the humidity in the summer though," Ava said.

"Especially compared to the dry air in California, the East Coast always feels like a sauna to me," Alexa said.

"I grew up in the south where humidity was a fact of life. I always laugh when Californians start complaining about the humidity when it reaches 12 percent." Jenna laughed.

"For sure! Californians don't know weather," Ava said.

The women checked into a two-bedroom suite in a lovely hotel. They unpacked and changed into skirts for dinner. They were mindful of looking professional in the nation's capital. California wardrobes, because of the heat and the culture, were a lot more casual. At 9:00 p.m. sharp, they arrived at Founding

Farmers to eat a light and clean, albeit late supper. Julia and Lauren joined them for dinner.

"Hi, Julia and Lauren!" Ava said.

Hugs were exchanged all around.

"Lauren, I feel like I've known you forever even though this is the first time we've actually met. You are even more beautiful than I expected."

Lauren blushed and said, "I am so glad I get to formally meet all of you. This is so much fun to be a part of your world-changing adventures. I love how you move so powerfully in praying and lining things up in the spirit, but you don't stop there. You then take practical steps to put God's kingdom into action. Thanks again for including me."

"You're very welcome. We love all that you add," Ava said.

"Julia says her nickname for you Ava is "Reaganista," Lauren said.

Ava looked at Julia and laughingly told Lauren, "That's a story for another day."

After they were seated and had ordered, Ava turned to Julia and Lauren and said, "I got both of you something special to honor you and to show you how unique you are."

The women smiled as Ava gave each of them a beautifully wrapped package.

"Julia, open yours first," Lauren urged.

"Okay, I will." Julia unwrapped her present and held up a beautiful gold necklace with a red stone wrapped ornately in gold.

"It's gorgeous, Ava! Thank you! I wear red a lot so this is perfect."

"You're very welcome. Look at the card with it. My friend owns a prophetic jewelry company called "Kingdom Creations," and she designs beautiful jewelry as a visible expression of the Lord's prophetic word over one's life. I was drawn to this necklace for you, and when I read the word, I knew it reflected your heart."

"Read it aloud, Julia," Alexa urged.

"Yes, please do," Jenna and Elle agreed.

Julia picked the rose-colored card from the box and read, "Jewels for the Journey Collection. 'Poured Out.' The Scripture is from Mark 14 where Mary poured out the alabaster vial of perfume over Jesus. The prophetic word says, 'Empty yourself before Me. Pour out the most precious things of life for My purposes. Risk the reproach of others to honor and love Me. Your extravagance toward me, though it mystifies others, honors Me. Fear not the grateful and passionate expression of your heart. I gave My life for you—is there anything worth holding from Me? Be a life poured out: in so doing, you will be remembered in eternity.'"

"That word is so perfect for Julia. It so describes the life she lives poured out for God," Lauren exclaimed.

"Thank you, Ava. I am honored and will cherish this gift," Julia said.

"You're welcome. I'm proud of you and what you're doing in your life. Your turn, Lauren."

The women all watched Lauren open her present. She pulled out a black-beaded chain with blue, green, and yellow beads interspersed with a blue, green, yellow, and black sparkly triangular pendant.

"It's beautiful!" Lauren squealed.

The ladies all admired the necklace while Lauren opened the card to read aloud, "This, too, is from Jewels for the Journey collection entitled 'Glory.' The scripture verse is Isaiah 60:1–3 where we are commanded to 'Arise, shine, for your light has come, and the glory of the Lord is risen upon you. See, darkness covers the earth and thick darkness is over the peoples, but the Lord rises upon you, and His glory appears over you. Nations will come to your light and kings to the brightness of your dawn," Lauren said.

"That is my favorite Scripture! The prophetic word is, 'My glory is on you. You carry it with you, and it shines through you. Rise up and shine no matter the circumstances. Rise up and shine so the darkness fades away and reveals the vitality of My life in you. Your light will draw many from the nations, for I have called every tribe and tongue, and by the light visible in you, the darkness over their lives will be dispelled. Know that I am with you and have anointed you. Arise, shine with the brightness of My glory.'

"That so describes Lauren! How thoughtful," Julia said.

"Thank you, Ava. This necklace is one of the best gifts I've been given, like a kiss from God," Lauren said.

"You're very welcome. He led me to get that one for you, so it's definitely a kiss," Ava said.

Their dinner arrived then, and as they ate, the conversation turned to their husbands and children. They made plans to meet up in the morning and then bid their good nights. The women from California were all tired after a long day of travel. They each called their husbands and children and went to bed to adjust their sleep schedule to the eastern time zone.

Chapter 5

❧◆❧

After a quick breakfast together, Jenna, Alexa, and Elle left the hotel to meet Lauren and Julia's chief of staff, Deborah Nelson, at the Hart Senate Building while Ava and Julia met at the Washington Monument to walk and talk together and enjoy the beautiful cherry blossom trees in the nation's capital. Ava was an avid walker. Julia was the only woman she knew who walked faster than she did. Ava was up for the challenge and had plans to ply Julia with questions so that Julia would exert more energy while speed walking and doing the majority of the talking.

Before Ava could launch into her questions, Julia asked Ava, "What is God showing you about today and what is your plan?"

"My plan for the meeting with the Appropriations Committee Senators is to talk about the identity, purpose, and destiny of the US and of the Republican and Democratic parties. The primary reason the parties have disagreed on how to appropriate spending is they haven't had a clear vision for our identity as a nation. Out of identity flows purpose and destiny, and necessarily, the money follows those priorities," Ava said.

"Seems simple yet profound."

"It is similar to how a family determines where to spend money. When a family understands its particular identity, whether the focus is a nice home, vacations, private school, or athletics, members can plan accordingly. Without a plan, spending occurs randomly and the parents can feel frustrated by not living the life they want and achieving the goals they want to. No matter the size of the budget, a plan based on the family's identity and purpose is key."

"That is exactly what goes wrong in the budget committee meetings. We don't have clear priorities, and therefore, we don't know where we want to live sacrificially. In addition, because we aren't focused on a national identity and priorities, everyone feels beholden to their subcommittee and constituents instead of the nation overall," Julia said.

"That's what the Lord instructed me to help with: identity, purpose, and destiny. He said you all would then be able to form a budget that is in line with the United States' God-given identity."

"Sounds perfect! Our meeting is this afternoon at 2:00 p.m. I told them to expect an out-of-the-box meeting where we would discuss our nation's priorities, and God would be at the center of the conversation. They know of your business and policy background and the work you've done with other politicians in the capitol and your focus on God. I think some were skeptical, but overall, we would all like to move forward. As you know, our backs are against the wall to submit a new budget that reflects a trillion dollars in cuts," Julia said. "Actual cuts, too, not just robbing Peter to pay Paul," Julia added.

They continued on in silence past the Jefferson Memorial and the line of blooming cherry trees. Ava was admiring all the monuments and reveling in the fact that the United States of America's forefathers had devised a constitution that was standing the test of time. She was convinced the US had strong roots and merely needed a course correction.

Chapter 6

❧⬥❧

J enna, Elle, and Alexa walked into the lobby of the Hart Senate Office Building. As promised, Lauren was waiting for them on the other side of the security checkpoint.

"Good morning, Ladies. I trust you slept well," Lauren said brightly.

"Good morning, Lauren," Elle said.

Hugs were exchanged all around. The women were dressed in business attire and blended in with the personnel on Capitol Hill.

"Let's go to Julia's office. Her chief of staff, Deborah, is waiting to let us in."

"You seem to know your way around the Hill, Lauren," Alexa said.

"I do. Julia asked me to be her personal intercessor when she became a senator. I come up here a couple times a week to pray through her offices. I sweep for bugs, the spiritual kind," Lauren said with a wink.

The ladies all laughed. The Capitol Hill offices were regularly swept for listening devices or "bugs" to be sure the senators and their staff were not being spied on. Most didn't know the importance of managing the spiritual environment as well. The women's morning assignment was to cleanse the spiritual atmosphere in the meeting rooms. This would facilitate hearing from God and remove any spirits of confusion and discord. They would accomplish this through worship and declarations.

"Here we are," Lauren said as she opened the door.

The door placard read "Senator Julia Thompson, California." The ladies entered the tastefully appointed offices. Julia's chief of staff was waiting just inside the door.

"Deborah, good to see you today. May I introduce Alexa Walker, Jenna Hunter, and Elle Clark. Ava Wellington will be in later this morning."

Handshakes and greetings were exchanged while Deborah said, "I've been looking forward to this week. I am hopeful that we will make some good inroads in the Committee on Appropriations."

Deborah was a petite, well-dressed woman in her mid-forties. She was very intelligent, well spoken, politically savvy, and carried a strong sense of justice. She was a great asset to lead Julia's team.

"We'll pray through our Senate office first, and then we'll go to the Capitol Building to pray through the room where the Appropriations Committee convenes," Lauren said.

"That's perfect," Deborah said. "Let me know if you need anything."

"Will do. Thanks again," Lauren said as she led the intercessors into Julia's private office.

Alexa set up her iPhone to play worship music in the room. She played "The Blessing" by Kari Jobe, Cody Carnes, and Elevation Worship. Instantly, God's presence flooded the room. The women began walking around, quietly worshipping. When they felt that the suite of rooms was saturated with love and the atmosphere of heaven, Lauren led them over to the Capitol Building and down the corridor to the US Senate Committee on Appropriations' room. The hallway was gorgeously tiled from floor to arched ceiling. It resembled a Roman building. The committee room was stately and large to accommodate the thirty-one senators on the committee, their staff, members of the press, and visitors. The center of the room had a large four-sided rectangular table with open space in the middle. It was surrounded by leather chairs for the senators and rows of staff chairs lined the outer walls.

The women looked at each other. Despite the beauty of the hallway and room, they were focused on the spiritual atmosphere.

"Feels like the previous meeting in here didn't go so well. I especially feel the darkness over there," Alexa said, gesturing to the corner farthest from the door they'd entered.

"You're right, Alexa. You feel the spirits. I see them. I see evil spirits of division, contention, and pride ensconced against the wall. They are not happy to see us. I think they've been there for a while. No wonder the committee keeps reaching an impasse after the subcommittees reach consensus," Elle said.

"Have you prayed in here before, Lauren?" Jenna asked.

"No. This is the first time, but I can see it needs to be a priority."

Alexa set up her iPhone.

"This calls for a breaker anointing to clear the room of darkness and infuse it with light."

Alexa chose the classic song "We Believe" by Brian and Jenn Johnson to transform the atmosphere. The women began worshipping their King.

Elle started laughing. "I just saw two big angels come in. When the demons saw them, they ran out shrieking. What made me laugh was the angels were wearing tuxedos, just like Ava's angels do. Very tough, yet formal warriors."

The women laughed at the image.

"Ava's angels are probably having a family reunion with their political cohorts," Jenna said.

"It does feel better in here," Alexa said.

Elle looked carefully around the room. "Yes, it's clean in here. Now let's fill it with God's presence, and the angels He sent can keep guard."

The intercessors walked back to the Hart Building to Julia's office and saw Ava and Julia talking with Julia's chief of staff, Deborah. Deborah had ordered Starbucks coffee for the women. She had investigated the ladies' favorite drinks and had them customized.

"Wow, Deborah. Hot mochas for Elle and Lauren, iced mocha for Ava, iced chai latte for Alexa, hot chai latte for me. Very impressive," Jenna said.

"Deborah is amazing. She makes me look like a genius around here," Julia said as she sipped her own iced mocha.

"Deborah, I feel like I have a prophetic word for you from God. Would you like to hear it?" Ava said.

Deborah looked surprised, but said, "Yes. Yes, I think I would."

She was a believer in Jesus Christ but didn't have personal experience with prophecy.

"Deborah, I hear the Lord saying that you are a keeper of time in God's kingdom. You carry the ability to synchronize the earth's chronological time with what heaven wants to release into the earth in a kairos moment. You may not be aware of it, but you function in it at work by 'sensing' what bills are ready to be put forth to the Senate for vote and by knowing who needs to meet with whom and when. It's pretty second nature to you, but the anointing is from the Lord, and it is important. I also saw you functioning in this anointing in your personal life. I saw you knowing just when to buy a new car or house or make airline reservations. Your life flows really smoothly because you cooperate with the timing of heaven," Ava said.

Deborah's jaw had dropped open. Ava had explained something she'd always wondered about; how she instinctively understood timing. Her husband had noticed her ability to flow through time and depended on her for investment decisions, timing of vacations, and even the timing of buying and selling of real estate.

Jenna chimed in and began prophesying over Deborah, "I see you are full of wisdom, just like Judge Deborah in the book of Judges in the Bible. You carry a strong sense of justice, and you carry the plumb line of God. The plumb line of God is what God drops from heaven as the absolute of right and wrong, moral integrity, true purity, and holiness. Purity is not just the absence of evil; it is the presence of what is right and good, what is lovely, what is love."

Julia was excited by what was spontaneously happening. She had described to Deborah what the ladies would be bringing to the senators by prophesying their identity, their purpose, and their call. Now, Deborah was experiencing firsthand what it felt like to be intimately known and loved by a good God and be empowered to walk in the uniqueness of whom she was called to be.

Elle said, "Deborah, I saw you praying and also talking to God about what you are supposed to do. Like Jenna said, you carry justice and wisdom, and because of that, I saw you asking God if you were supposed to be working in the judicial side of government. In fact, I saw you asking Him about the Supreme Court, but I heard God say you're exactly where you're supposed to be. He has gifted you with wisdom to help write the laws to bring justice and given you the timing anointing to help bring it to pass."

Deborah was crying now as she listened to the word of the Lord over her life. The ladies brought so many answers to questions she had been asking God. Prior to working in the Senate, she had worked in the Supreme Court. She looked inquisitively at Julia.

Julia laughed and said, "No, I didn't tell them you worked in the Supreme Court. They got that information from God. When Ava said she had a word for you, I started recording it for you so that you can hear it again and remember what was spoken over you. You may also want to transcribe it. I, personally, carry all of my prophetic words in my computer and on my phone, so when I'm feeling discouraged and disconnected from God, I can read them and remember who God says I am, what He has for me, and feel His heart championing me.

"Thanks so much. I'm going to take a moment to compose myself," Deborah said moving toward the bathroom door.

"Great. See you in a moment," Julia said.

"And that's how it's done," Alexa said as she high-fived Ava.

"That's exactly why we're here," Ava agreed.

Chapter 7

⊷◈⊶

J ulia's staff and interns began to crowd into her office. The men and women sat on the various couches and chairs and around the conference table. A few of the men brought folding chairs for the remainder of the staff. Julia introduced the women from Northern California and then turned the meeting over to Ava.

"Good morning. It's so nice to meet all of you. I have a deep respect for the work you all do for our country. Thank you," Ava said, smiling at each one assembled. "Julia asked me to talk with you all this morning, mostly to equip you in spiritual matters that will aid your work in government. The first thing I want to talk about is who God is. This may be redundant for some of you, but I want to start with a good foundation and get us all on the same page. God is good. All the time and He is only good. He is loving. Jesus is the exact representation of God the Father. Jesus said,

'If you've seen Me, you've seen the Father.' Anything you see in the Old Testament that is not consistent with the life of Jesus is not who God is. It's an inferior revelation of God's heart.

"The primary message of the Old Testament is that man is a sinner in need of a Savior. The point of the law in the Old Testament era is that man is not capable of keeping the law. The law revealed sin and the need for forgiveness. It all pointed to the love affair God has with restoring man to the original glory and relationship He created for them. The primary message of the New Testament era is the revelation that those who receive Jesus's sacrifice for the world are forgiven of sin and saved by grace. We receive the mercy of God because Jesus paid for our sin and gives us a new nature—a nature that is prone toward righteousness instead of sinfulness. God's heart toward the world is to extend mercy. Mercy triumphs over judgment. The kindness of God leads to repentance, and where sin abounds, God's grace abounds even more. God always encourages, always brings hope. Even His corrections bring life, encouragement, and the grace to change. As His kids, our assignment now is to bring hope and to disciple nations with the love of God and to be faithful with the gifting God has given us."

Ava paused for a drink of water and gauged the reaction among the staffers in the room.

"Our end-time theology has to be victorious. We have to be releasers of hope. Throughout church history, the end-time theology beliefs have ranged from overcoming and being victorious in the earth to a theology of the world going up in flames and the church needing to be rescued/raptured. God doesn't intend for believers to be rescued. He intends for us to know who He is, who we are in Him, bring a revelation of Him as a good Father to people, and to bring heaven's solutions to earth's problems. If not us, then whom? When the church started believing that the world was going to get so dark with sin and trouble, many believers abdicated their authority and shirked their duty by pulling back from business, education, politics, Hollywood, and the media. Those realms, without lots of believers in them, did get darker as evidenced by the massive scandal that has recently rocked our world." Ava waited to let her message sink in.

A few were nodding in agreement.

"Who you believe God is to you is who He will be through you. Julia was placed in this office by God for such a time as this. Each one of you, as one who works really hard to help her, is also placed here for such a time as this. You are able to shift the direction of the nation, to partner with God's plans for the United States. If you aren't settled in your heart that God is good and loves people, I recommend you read, *God Is Good: He's Better Than You Think* and listen to "Enduring Faith" both by my pastor Bill Johnson. He goes in-depth about what I just talked about. Many people get tripped up by the judgments they see in the Old Testament, and they then don't trust and understand God's heart of love and redemption. We are each one accountable to God for how we live our lives, but when we understand that He is a good Father, cheering us on to use our giftings well, we can run our race with integrity and joy.

"Right now, I want to take the next fifteen minutes to have Elle, Jenna, and Alexa prophesy God's heart over each one of you so that you can know how the God of the universe feels about you specifically. He made each one of you unique with distinct identities and giftings. I can talk all I want about these principles, but until you tangibly experience His presence and His love, it can just be religion and theory. I also want you to listen to how Jesus sees the others because you will then view your colleagues from the lens of heaven."

The women prophesied over each staff member individually. When they finished, there was not a dry eye in the room, even for the men present.

"Anyone want to share their experience?" Ava asked.

A young man named Matt raised his hand. "You all read my mail! You spoke of things about me that I dreamed about as a little boy. I feel so encouraged to pursue more of who I am and what I am called to do. I also didn't realize how well we all work together as a team in this office. Some of the personality traits that I saw as quirky in myself and others are giftings we need as a whole team to accomplish our jobs. I also saw that areas I am lacking in, others are strong in. God really is very strategic in how He puts people together. I also want to get to know God better. I've never felt His love so clearly."

Julia spoke up. "You articulated that really well, Matt. Next week, I want to do some team building and listen to God together about our unique purpose and vision in the Senate." Julia gestured to Ava to continue leading the meeting.

Ava said, "I don't know how familiar each of you is with the spiritual realm and how it impacts the natural realm, but I'll explain how it operates and how we can cooperate with heaven's plans. In the beginning, when God created people, He created them for the express purpose of being in close relationship with them. God is sovereign, meaning He possesses ultimate power. However, because He wanted to give people (and angels) the free will to choose to love Him or the ability to not pick relationship with Him, He gave people the freedom to both elect Him and to choose good or evil. If God were to control us or not give us freedom to choose, we would just be puppets. He designed us to need freedom and need the ability to make our own choices. He was willing to allow us the freedom to not love Him because true love has to be chosen with true freedom. He gave every one ever born the freedom to choose to do good or evil. And He gave us the opportunity for the consequences for our choices to exist. He encourages us to love Him and to aspire toward righteousness and goodness because it brings a harvest of reward in our lives and for those around us. He also loves us so much and loves freedom that He lets us partner with evil. As a loving Father, His heart hurts when He sees the consequences we reap upon others and ourselves when we choose brokenness because of our own woundedness, our choices, or lies we're believing. He is always with us, and as we come to Him requesting help, He, in His infinite wisdom, helps us and parents us. This is all done through relationship. Love and relationship are His highest priorities."

Ava took a sip of her iced mocha and then continued, "That is what it looks like on an individual level. Where it starts to get complicated is on a global level. He gave freedom to all 7.7-plus billion people on the planet. But not everyone is free because of the choices that other people make. God's heart aches for the babies who are aborted, for the children who are abused by the very people who are supposed to be their protectors, for the slaves in modern-day society, for the victims of deranged school shooters, for the victims of dictators like Stalin, Hitler, Saddam Hussein, for victims of terrorist attacks, racism, and people stuck in poverty. And His heart aches for His children who perpetrate such evil. God has had a plan for redemption from before the foundation of the world. His plan begins with Jesus's death on the cross and resurrection — that all people who accept Him as their personal Savior are forgiven and get a spirit that awakens with a new nature prone toward choosing good. God then empowers these believers with His authority and power to bring His kingdom to earth. These believers are equipped to cooperate with heaven. That is not to say that other people who are not believers in Jesus Christ cannot also tap into God's plans for discipling nations simply because everyone is created in the image of God.

"God has a few primary objectives for this earth. First, He is looking for relationship with His children. Secondly, He is looking for His children to disciple nations, to make earth look like the government and freedom and peace and love of heaven. God chooses to work on earth through His children and His angels. He doesn't want to have Jesus come back again to rescue a planet steeped in darkness. His plan is for His children who know Him to bring light and make earth like heaven. Then Jesus will return. God has given us all the tools we need. Our tools and weapons are declarations to create, just like our Father: worship, wisdom, love, our creative minds, art, business, innovation, and many others. As we go forward, the angels help us. When we make a declaration, the angels go make it come to pass. The demonic realm opposes us. The demonic needs the agreement of people, just like the angelic realm needs the agreement of people to proceed. As people, when we walk in forgiveness, love, faith, hope, and honor, we empower the angelic to accomplish God's heart. When people walk in fear, bitterness, hatred, unforgiveness, offense, wrath, strife, division, sin, greed, and dishonor, they empower the demonic realm to further their kingdom goals of stealing, killing, and destroying. This is particularly important in the political arena. When you don't agree with someone, it is critical to still treat him or her with honor.

"In order for us to move forward, I think we need to take a few minutes to forgive all the world leaders for the egregious sin that's been exposed recently. We have to forgive them so that we ourselves can be free from bitterness. They each have or had the individual choice before death to repent to God and get right with Him."

Ava led them through a prayer to forgive the perpetrators of evil and release them from the Senate staffers' judgments.

"Everyone feel better?"

The staff nodded as they contemplated what Ava was speaking about.

Ava continued, "The demonic realm has been very strategic in furthering its agenda to bring perversion and to separate people from God and each other. One of the objectives is to get people trapped in bondage to things such as fear, anxiety, sexual sin, alcohol, drugs, gossip, hate, pornography, poverty, bitterness, greed, debt, power mongering, satanic worship, and corruption. When the enemy gets a person in bondage, that person is much less effective in bringing God's purposes and plans about.

"The enemy has a much smaller spiritual force than the angelic host, but they have leveraged their forces in a few effective ways. Spiritual forces have a hierarchal structure similar to our nation's armed forces: a leadership structure at the top and many soldiers who implement the strategies. The higher up in leadership a soldier goes, the more influence and power he wields. Same with the angelic and demonic structures.

"The demonic has used the spiritual airways to control regions and has positioned their influence at or near the top of the mountains of society. The airwaves operate both in the natural through media and communication and also like silent radio stations broadcasting thoughts to all in the region. In the case of the spiritual airwaves, all people hear the thoughts subconsciously, although the more spiritually alert will hear the thoughts consciously. There are both demonic and angelic airwaves operating in every region. Which one is more dominant is dependent upon the believers.

"Prayer, worship, and righteousness help control the spiritual airwaves with the message of heaven and love. People have the choice to be influenced positively or negatively by what is being broadcast in the airwaves. They choose by being intentional regarding their beliefs, their core values, their worldview, and by taking every thought captive that doesn't line up with their beliefs. The Bible illustrates this principle where the Apostle Paul teaches in 2 Corinthians 10:3-5, 'For though we walk in the flesh, we do not war according to the flesh. For the weapons of our warfare are not carnal but mighty in God for pulling down strongholds, casting down arguments and every high thing that exalts itself against the knowledge of God, bringing every thought into captivity to the obedience of Christ.' If people in a region don't recognize the arguments coming through the airwaves, they will adjust their beliefs to incorporate these new thoughts. The way to guard against that is to examine and discard beliefs that don't line up with Scripture and a biblical worldview."

Deborah spoke up. "I've experienced hearing the spiritual airwaves on different issues working here in Washington, DC. I've always been a firm believer in traditional marriage being between one man and one woman. A couple months before the Supreme Court was to announce their ruling on gay marriage in June 2015, I was walking outside enjoying the sunshine. All of a sudden, a soundtrack of thoughts that I knew weren't my own started running through my head. I heard, 'It won't hurt anything if gay people marry. Nothing will really change; after all, they love each other. It's not worth fighting about; why can't people just be happy. You're not really loving if you don't allow other people to get married; people should be free to choose whom they love.' I knew at that point that everyone in DC was hearing the same thing, including the justices, and that unless the individual justices took those thoughts captive, compared them to biblical truth, and discarded them, what they were hearing in the airwaves was going to be their belief, and the justices would rule accordingly. Which is precisely what happened."

"Exactly," Ava said. "Paul instructed taking every thought captive in a militant fashion to discard the thought because of how destructive the thought would become. The demonic influence over the airwaves in this country has increased dramatically in the past seventy years. The primary reason is because the plumb line of the Word of God lost influence through the public school system and through the increase of media. When young people stopped being taught scriptural core values, the demonic gained a foothold into changing mindsets. It's a very slippery slope. People believe their thoughts are just evolving toward freedom of expression and being "woke" and that those who disagree are full of hate. Incidentally, those prideful thoughts originated in the airwaves too. A very concrete example is sexuality. God designed sexuality to be fun and pleasurable and bonding within the covenant of marriage. God designed the brain to emit bonding and protective hormones when people are sexually intimate. He created the man and woman to enjoy each other sexually and bond to each other emotionally, for a lifetime. Within this covenant, sex is safe and amazing. Outside of this covenant, sex is a perversion and open to demonic influence. Outside of covenant, sex hurts people emotionally because it still creates soul ties — soul ties that were designed to be formed for one person for a lifetime. When a man has multiple sexual partners, multiple soul ties are formed stretching him and hurting his heart. Even after he moves on, in the spirit, a bond still connects him to previous partners, and unless the soul tie is broken in the spirit, he loses part of himself. Additionally, this soul tie can be created whether a person is physically intimate with another or through merely viewing pornography or engaging in romantic or sexual fantasy. Multiple soul ties reduce the ability to successfully bond to a spouse."

At this point, Julia interjected, "I agree with you. It's like sexual perversion has increased and is on a continuum. Sex outside of marriage was considered risqué in the 1950s. Free love in the 1960s didn't include homosexuality, the 1970s and 1980s increased promiscuity, and homosexuality became more mainstream in the 1990s and 2000s. The book *Fifty Shades of Grey* in the 2010s pushed the idea of sexual abuse being acceptable as a form of erotica. Where does sexual culture go from here?"

"Exactly. We've seen recently with the exposure of some of the world's elites the absolute sexual depravity and horror of rape, torture, and satanic ritual sacrifice of children. To get a sexual high, what used to satisfy is no longer enough. We can't point the finger at the elites, who with enough resources and power went down the devil's rabbit hole of sexual abomination, without realizing that without the grace of God, there go I. What about the people who watched but didn't participate and didn't report the heinous activities? We have, in recent history, seen the Nazis slaughter more than six million Jews and other people. If we think that the now cultural norms in our society of sex outside of marriage, homosexuality, and transgenderism didn't contribute to where the elites went with pedophilia, sex trafficking, drinking of adrenochrome, and the satanic slaughter of children, we're kidding ourselves."

Ava continued, "Sin is sin and hurts us, sometimes beyond repair. If we truly repent, God will help us restore and heal our people and land. When the church hasn't adequately explained to the world that sexual sin is inspired by the demonic, is a temptation to be ruled over and not someone's actual identity or birthright, people have no way of getting free. Instead, they are trapped in the pain and consequences that come along with partnering with the demonic and don't understand why their hearts hurt so much." Ava looked at Jenna then for her silent opinion regarding if Julia's staff was able to hear and comprehend the depth of what Ava was saying.

She knew the topic was controversial, and listening to Ava was often akin to drinking from a fire hose.

After seeing Jenna's nod, Ava continued, "That's exactly how the demonic inspired suggestions change culture if it is not anchored in how God sees. And people get more and more wounded in their souls and use more alcohol, drugs, and other escapes to numb their pain of not being bonded in a healthy manner and to get a sexual high. People are created to know and be known by God and through other intimate relationships. Perversion hampers the expression of true freedom. Ironically enough, the demonic entices people toward behavior, in the pursuit of the guise of freedom, which only increases bondage. Same strategy as the garden of Eden.

"The truth is homosexuality and other sexual perversions are not the result of a God-given identity or about love but rather is the acting upon of sexual temptation or appetite. Speaking this is not expressing rejection, hatred, or a lack of love. It is truth, and truth will set people free.

"I'm sure this may have brought up somethings you each want to get right with God about. I don't want to point out sin, brokenness, and ungodly soul ties without also providing the opportunity for repentance and freedom. I also don't want to embarrass anyone, so we're going to take a few minutes privately to repent. You're welcome to join us if you want or just sit quietly. Everyone, please close your eyes. If you want, you can say aloud quietly the following prayer. 'Father, I repent for all manner of sexual sin. I repent for not following Your plan for healthy sexuality through covenant marriage. I repent for sex outside of marriage, homosexuality, viewing pornography, adultery, and any other sexual sin. Please forgive me.'"

To Ava's surprise, everyone joined her and prayed aloud quietly.

"And now, let's break all ungodly soul ties. These are soul ties that are formed through sin. Repeat the following prayer for as many people as you need to. 'Father, I break ungodly soul ties with "person's name." I send back what's his/hers covered in the blood of Jesus, and I take back what's mine covered in the blood of Jesus.' Now clap your hands once to break the soul tie. Repeat after me to break soul ties with anyone you've viewed through pornography or sexual fantasy. 'Father, I repent for viewing and engaging in pornography and sexual fantasy. I break ungodly soul ties with everyone I've viewed in pornography and sexual fantasy. I send back what's theirs covered in the blood of Jesus, and I take back what's mine covered in the blood of Jesus.' And clap once."

The room immediately felt brighter and lighter. Ava looked at Elle to confirm what she was feeling. Elle nodded toward the angels she saw who were ministering to Julia's staff. A peace descended upon the office.

When Ava sensed the work of God completed, she continued, "Different cities and regions of the country have identities and destinies that God has ordained and that the enemy has tried to highjack. Staying with the theme of sexual immorality, the demonic has leveraged the airways for sexual perversion in San Francisco, California. As a person comes into that region, they will be assaulted with thoughts and suggestions of perverse sexuality. They may think what they are subconsciously hearing is their own thoughts. If they recognize the suggestions as untrue because of a personal core value of purity, they will be unaffected by what is being broadcast in the airwaves. If they don't reject the impure thoughts, they will take the suggestions on as truth and adjust to make those their own values, whether they personally act on them or not. San Francisco actually has an identity given from God for being a city that extends mercy. Mercy means to extend kindness, forgiveness, or benevolence.

"However, mercy can be unsanctified if it's extended without the help and expectation of the broken to become whole or pure. Jesus was the perfect example. He extended mercy to the woman caught in adultery who the religious of the day wanted to punish by stoning to death. Jesus forgave her, stayed the consequences, yet admonished her to go and sin no more. That's sanctified mercy. He knew the brokenness she was experiencing because of her actions and wanted her heart to be healed and be whole. Jesus's heart for us is for us to be healed. Therefore, the commandment to go and sin no more.

"As the church, we have to make it clear that we love people but not the sin that leads to bondage. We've let the culture preempt our voice and call us haters because we call homosexuality sin. Silence is unsanctified mercy and hurts generations who have normalized sexual sin as identity and for love instead of a temptation and appetite to be managed with God's help.

"Unsanctified mercy creates more brokenness and has no path to healing. San Francisco has a mandate from God to heal the brokenhearted and to set the captives free. Isaiah prophesied in chapter 61 what that would look like. The demonic enemy has co-opted the purpose of San Francisco. I believe when the people of San Francisco see Jesus for whom He really is as the lover of their souls and partner with His plan for freedom, they will lead the world in showing sanctified mercy to the poor, the broken, and the downtrodden. In addition, the resources of neighboring Cupertino, California, will be available to partner with to change the world.

"There are obviously other cities who have leadership mandates from God on them. Yet when people move into the cities to work in leadership there, unless they stay rooted in their core biblical values, they will begin to partner with what the demonic is broadcasting over the airwaves. The key to not being affected is to have core values established, know what truth is, know what God says, and disregard anything that doesn't line up with that truth.

"Dawna DeSilva of Bethel Church taught us how to discern and shift atmospheres. For example, if a person is a 'feeler' in the spiritual realm, he/she will sense what the enemy is sending out through the airwaves as an emotion as well as by hearing thoughts. Emotions have to be taken captive because emotions feel more real than a thought can and extra care has to be taken to be vigilant in learning how to function with discernment gifts. When a person who is feeling tormented by an emotion that feels directed at him/her, if he/she releases the opposite in a declaration into the airwaves of the city, it is akin to a counter punch to the enemy. More ground will be taken for God with a counter punch, and eventually, the enemy will stop tormenting people because he loses so much ground through the counterattack. There is no need to come against the demonic directly; merely by releasing God's thoughts aloud, the angelic will be empowered to take down the demonic in the region."

Ava went on to explain discernment in more detail and then concluded with an example in prayer.

"It's pretty simple in practical application. For example, if I am feeling afraid or anxious, I will go to God and ask Him what He says about my situation. Often, an attack is not only against me personally but also against my city. In some cases, I may remember a prophetic word of what He said He was going to do. When I know the truth of what God says, I know the emotion of fear or anxiety is a lie from the enemy. So I will say, 'I release peace and the perfect love of God to myself and over my city.' That's my counter punch. Scripture says that the perfect love of God casts out all fear.

"We all have authority over the city we live in. We have varying degrees of authority over our nation and our world. After I make a declaration, I will immediately 'feel' better and will notice the fear or anxiety is gone. Because I discerned what was going on in the spiritual realm, I was able to change what was going out over the spiritual airwaves in my city. Now perfect love and peace is being broadcast. If I travel to another city and I discern negative airwaves, I'll pray but I also ask God to have the Christians who live there pray in agreement.

"There's a process in each of our individual lives of getting healed, knowing truth, and being delivered of all demonic influence. I remember after a lot of growth in God regarding trusting Him the first time a demon of fear showed up at my window, and it no longer had agreement inside of me. I was fully delivered and had a transformed mind regarding trust and God's perfect love. Freedom is a process for each of us. I never make decisions when I feel afraid. Instead, I get alone with God and get aware of His presence and dream with Him. That doesn't mean that everything always works out perfectly, but I follow the direction I feel His peace in.

"We just got into some deep stuff. Deborah is recording our sessions, so feel free to go back and listen to this again if it was new to you. Let's take a ten-minute break. Elle,

Alexa, Jenna, and I will take personal questions during that time," Ava said. "When we reconvene, I'll talk about the second demonic strategy of targeting the leadership in the realms of society."

Chapter 8

➤⬢❲

Most of the staff had questions for the women and also had to return emails, so the break stretched on longer than Ava had planned because the business of government never stops. When they finally were able to begin again, Julia prayed and asked the Lord to bless them with wisdom and understanding and more of His manifest presence in the room. Then she invited Ava to continue the meeting.

Ava looked around before beginning. She saw a large new angel that had joined the gathering of angelic already assembled in the room. She asked God what the purpose was for the new angel. The Lord spoke to her that the angel was a nations' discipling angel. One that would aid in the explanation of what Jesus meant to disciple nations. His other role was to be a scribe for any godly assignments that would be declared that would need to be set in motion by the angelic realm. That revelation greatly encouraged Ava as she began speaking.

"The second strategy of the demonic targets the leadership of the mountains of influence. If the enemy can get agreement from a corporate leader, a top Hollywood director, an influential politician, or an education curriculum writer, he can leverage his power to bring more destruction to the world. Or the enemy can give a person a leadership role who has traded his/her soul on the trading floors of hell for power, fame, and wealth. The enemy can then shift how we perceive life and create a new normal—one that is darker and more evil. I am not saying that the leaders in the different arenas in our nation are evil. I am saying that if their thoughts and values are not calibrated with God's views, the enemy can use their influence to multiply his purposes. There are varying degrees to which this happens. That is why God says that to whom much is given, much is required. When we have influence, we have to be sure to steward it correctly because many people are impacted by the views of their leaders. The Founding Fathers understood this and took their power seriously. They knew they were accountable for how they stewarded their influence. We can look at examples of leaders throughout history where the enemy inspired a destructive thought process which the world leader partnered with, like Adolf Hitler, which resulted in the slaughter of millions of people. As we're all aware, we've recently had a large number of leaders arrested worldwide for horrific crimes against humanity."

"That sounds gruesome, like we are already losing the planet. What is the solution?" Deborah asked.

"Remember the movie *It's a Wonderful Life* with Jimmy Stewart? He wondered what the purpose of his life was about and was discouraged by his seemingly small existence. The angel showed him how darkness could not encroach because he was light there."

"Yes. I love that movie," Deborah said.

"New leaders have been elected and hired worldwide and have an opportunity to bring God's righteousness to earth. Christians who carry and walk with the Holy Spirit bring light into regions as do unbelievers who choose love and righteous behavior. Darkness is automatically displaced or held at bay when people walk with the blueprints of heaven. Unbelievers can also tap into the strategies and creativity of heaven to disciple nations because they're also made in the image of God. When there is light, God's purposes are accomplished, and people have more opportunity to choose Him when they see His goodness released. God is raising leaders up whom He has refined to be placed into all realms of society. They will join and also replace some of the leaders already in the mountains. He showed me three waves of people being put in place. The first wave was the training of many leaders. The second wave is currently being released and accounts for hundreds of thousands of people around the world bringing light. The third wave consists of millions of people over the next twenty to thirty years. These people play a key role in God's end-time discipling nations strategy. The landscape of many nations will look significantly better over the next few decades."

"When you say 'disciple nations,' what does that practically look like?" Deborah asked.

"That's a really good question. Biblically, the primary consideration for being considered a sheep nation is recognizing and honoring Israel and the Jewish people as God's chosen. In addition, it means that, overall, a nation's citizens are healthy and living productive lives. It means that crime is low. People are safe, and families have healthy relationships. People have the freedom to pursue their dreams and their God-given talents in a way that brings life to others. It is where people can work hard to make a living for themselves, where innovation and creativity can flourish in all realms of society, where people have hope and a vision for their future and for the generations, where people have freedom to worship God, and where people are not oppressed. This doesn't mean that every idea is encouraged. There are always moral absolutes of what is right and what is wrong. There are consequences and harvests to be reaped. God is not afraid of people's choices. He didn't hide the forbidden tree in a back corner of the garden of Eden. It was right in front. True freedom is the ability and right to say yes or no to something. When a nation is healthy, the people are healthy and are making good choices to take care of themselves in prospering spirit, soul, and body. Their communication is healthy. They are not using drugs and alcohol excessively to self-medicate emotional pain. Instead, they have tools to work through situations so that their souls are healthy instead of pain being stuffed. It means that marriages are healthy where both people are powerful, and one is not controlling or manipulating the other. It means that children are loved and nurtured by a mother and a father so that the children's needs are met. It means that generations of people are not living in poverty because of hopelessness, brokenness, discrimination, and not having opportunity to thrive. It means that all races and classes of people are respected and not discriminated against. It means that women are respected and given equal opportunity as men in a society and that men are also rightfully respected. Discipling nations happens at every level of society in all realms of society. Creativity, innovation, self-control, and self-responsibility abound. It means that neighbors help neighbors, and people in cities respond to the needs of people in their cities.

"Churches and ministries of compassion are uniquely gifted for discipling their cities. People are drawn to the Truth that is Jesus, and the Truth sets them free. Discipling people has to happen in a relationship, not at a government level.

"Government is not equipped or gifted to help meet people's needs because people change and grow out of relationship with healthy people and also because government gets bogged down in the bureaucratic process and is less effective but at a much greater financial cost. Our nation in recent decades has looked to government to father them. Fathers provide identity, protection, and provision. It's not government's job to provide identity or provision to people. It is, however, government's job to provide safety and protection. When government tries to father a nation, the people are not empowered to operate the way they've been created and actually lose more freedom and rights.

"Churches were actually designated by God to bless and serve their city and the people in it. Churches are called to carry a benevolent movement: to meet spiritual, physical, and soul needs for people in their community. Churches have the tools to help end cycles of poverty by dealing with and healing the root causes of poverty cycles in people. Government is not equipped or called to help people solve generational cycles. Churches are able to rehabilitate people and bring true change. Government statistics show that when government operates in benevolence instead of churches, it costs a tremendous amount of money with very little change accomplished. And then people become dependent on government aid," Ava said.

Deborah nodded in understanding, so she continued, "When God puts people into areas of influence in society, He is actually asking them to "father" or "mother" the people they influence. A good father or mother protects their children, empowers them to operate in their giftings, loves them, helps them grow, and learn and mature."

Ava gestured to Alexa to turn on the music.

"What I want to do now is take the next fifteen minutes to get into God's presence and rest. We call this "soaking." The Lord is going to refresh each of us, take away our burdens, and give us fresh vision. Some of you will get downloads from heaven where God will show you strategies. Others will just rest and spend time with Father God. You can lean back in your chairs and close your eyes or even find a spot on the floor and lay down. Do whatever is comfortable for you. Then we are going to come back together as a group and prophesy as a staff the identity and purpose of the United States."

Julia told her staff, "If you've never done this before, just clear your mind of any problems and worries and focus on God. He will fill you with peace. It's okay if you fall asleep; we call that "sloaking," and God will meet you in that place."

Alexa turned on "Captured" by Alberto and Kimberly Rivera. Beautiful music soon filled the room as they all got comfortable and closed their eyes. Ava didn't set a timer; she knew Holy Spirit would cue her at the end of fifteen minutes to keep them on schedule.

As Ava soaked, she reflected on how lost the nation had gotten. The Founding Fathers got their courage and direction from relationship with Jesus and from sermons preached by their pastors. It was no surprise that, presently, the nation's government was drowning in debt, and leaders at all levels of government were mired in conflict over the direction of the nation and how to get there. She sighed and exchanged the worries of the world for the peace and rest of God.

The room became very peaceful as Julia's staff members truly began resting. God's presence filled the room, and the angels quietly ministered to the people in the room. Ava saw some angels touching and activating the spiritual connective points in the peoples' heads and hearts. As those parts of the brain and heart were stimulated, the people rested even more deeply, and fear, doubt, and mocking left. When fifteen minutes had passed, Holy Spirit gently nudged Ava back to alertness. Ava stretched and asked Alexa to turn off the worship music.

Deborah was the first to speak.

She said, "That was wonderful! I haven't been that relaxed in years."

The others thoughtfully agreed.

"People who incorporate a soaking time with Jesus into their day have more energy, more focus, and are more hopeful. Companies who encourage their employees to "nap" are actually tapping into a strategy of heaven where God releases inventions, solutions, and strategies to people," Ava said.

"That is such a good idea. We're going to start implementing that here," Julia said.

She looked at Deborah, and they agreed to come up with a time each day where they could connect with God as a staff.

"Okay, now that we are full of God's presence and thinking from His perspective, we are going to ask Him what the unique identity and purpose of the United States is. Then we will take this and present it to the Senate Committee on Appropriations," Ava said.

Jenna was poised to write the ideas on the white board at the front of the conference room. She titled a few categories: "Identity of US," "Purpose of US," and "Strengths of US."

Ava prayed, "Holy Spirit, I ask You to show us the purpose, identity, and strengths of our great nation. Thank you for giving us the mind of Christ that we can see from heaven's perspective. Amen." She looked at Julia's assembled staff members and encouraged them to call out what they thought.

One by one, they began to speak. As they did, Jenna organized their thoughts into a list on the white board.

Jenna then shared the compilation aloud. "The United States is called to be a city on the hill—a beacon of hope and freedom. We are called to be a model of excellence and innovation, and from excellence, we will have influence in the world. We have a missionary call to bring the Gospel of Jesus Christ to the world. This is not fulfilled through government but through the citizens prospering. We have a missionary call to bring freedom to the oppressed in the world. This has to be done strategically because, at any given time, we have finite time and resources. We are called to be visionaries. As we have vision for our future, other nations draft off of our progress. We are called to be a protector of human rights. This will often be accomplished by church groups. As a government, we can empower the church to help the poor and oppressed of the world."

Jenna paused as she sipped some water and then continued, "What we have so far corresponds to some things I've written down that Arthur Burk of Sapphire Leadership Group explains about the identity of America. Let me read to you some notes from Arthur's teachings. 'We all agree that the United States is most energized and driven when we either have an enemy or a positive objective. We need either something tangible to overcome or a vision to accomplish. Outside of a worthy goal to achieve, the US often misguidedly spends money on random, unproductive ventures because we are driven to move forward to solve problems. We need to have leadership who understands how to partner with God in hearing from heaven what our goals and direction are. We need an ideological leader — a man or woman who "fathers" this nation. A good spiritual father articulates vision or purpose and, in the process, leads, empowers, protects, and provides identity and resources. We as a nation are called to dream, to see beyond the horizon, to walk in faith, and believe in the impossible. We are called to be dynamic innovators, to come up with ideas, and implement them with excellence. We are called as a nation to give resources, leadership, vision, help, love, the Gospel, creativity, and freedom to the nations of the world with wisdom. We are called to see and prepare for the future. We are also called to prophesy identity and destiny of other nations of the world. We are not called to rule or dominate other nations. That is their job.'"

"Thanks, Jenna, for putting all of that so succinctly," Ava said.

"Overall, I see two main themes in what we came up with," Julia said. "First, we have a call to lead our nation in freedom, in vision, in innovation. The second call is to help lead the world in these areas. I see a few weaknesses or obstacles that can hinder our purpose. Now that we've uncovered and are eliminating the infiltration of the deep state against our nation, it's no longer the biggest threat. The first problem is the very real threat of foreign nations, primarily from both China and the UK, against our nation. The defense of our nation needs to be robust in order that freedom and vision may reign. The second major weakness, no less urgent, is the ongoing state of our finances. The treasonous actions of previous leaders through laundering money through foreign aid and insider trading, the deep state's central banking plot to control and decimate world economies, our debt, our annual deficit, our highly taxed society, and our financial responsibilities can all derail our role in the world and potentially contribute to the ultimate collapse of our nation."

"I agree. The financial picture and threat of a global takeover attempt are the two main threats to this nation and ultimately to the world because the US provides such a leadership role in the world. We have to get our finances in order so that we may accomplish our purpose," Ava said.

"In addition, we need serious campaign reform, politician term limits, financial monitoring and accountability in our leaders' personal finances, elimination of lobbying by either US or foreign actors whether corporate or governmental, and strictly enforced consequences for all politicians who have engaged in these practices. I, in cooperation with other senators, will be drafting bills to these effects," Julia said.

"That's critical going forward. Good job taking the lead for action in all of that," Ava said.

"This is a good place to break for lunch," Julia said.

She thanked her staff for their participation as they left for lunch.

Deborah said, "Lauren made chicken fruit salad croissant sandwiches to bless you all, and I ordered some additional lunch items for us. It's such a beautiful day outside. Why don't we take our lunch outside for a picnic?"

"Wow! Thanks so much, Lauren! Is there anything you can't do?" Ava said.

Chapter 9

❦❖❧

As the seven ladies settled in and began eating their delicious lunch, Ava asked, "If we could name the identity of the United States in one word, what would it be?"

"This seems obvious, but I'd say it's freedom," Deborah said.

"I'd agree. Our nation from the very beginning was designed for freedom, and we've always fought for freedom, for ourselves and for others. And I think we're different from other nations in that regard. Freedom is more of a priority for Americans than any other nation," Julia said.

"So our God-given identity is freedom. And therefore, our purpose in the world is what? To be a beacon of freedom? To bring freedom to the world?" Deborah said.

"First, I think we're to actually become free ourselves—free in our finances and not slaves to debt, horrific taxes, and the corrupt central banking system, free in the sense of having self-control in managing our money well and understanding our limitations, free in not discriminating against any person for any reason. I think because of our unique identity for freedom, we don't want to rule other nations. We want to help them achieve freedom for themselves, and then we want to exit, unlike other nations who want to fold other nations into their kingdom," Julia said.

"I think we have to actually achieve sovereignty over ourselves before we can fully walk in our identity or our purpose. We've been slaves to debt—slaves to other people controlling and limiting us because of how we've mishandled our resources and how we've been oppressed by the few banking families in the last couple hundred years who corrupted our nation to be beholden to them financially. Thankfully, we're in the process of extricating ourselves from that tangled web. And may our posterity never again include our being financial slaves," Deborah said.

"Amen!" Elle, Jenna, and Alexa chorused and then giggled.

"In our God-given identity of freedom, I'd say our purpose is to be free, and from that place, through modeling and discipling, help other nations in the world to be free. Our actions would have to be carefully thought out regarding our policies going forward, or we'll end up in bondage ourselves again," Ava said.

"We've focused a lot on the financial ramifications of slavery, but I'd also say that we've gotten ourselves far from freedom because of the misconstrued sexual identity, sexual practices, and abortion in this nation," Elle said.

"I completely agree. The enemy sure has had a heyday in our land. Sexual freedom that doesn't line up with what God says about sex is not freedom at all," Julia said.

"The American people need such wisdom in electing our public officials. Election integrity, term limits, financial accountability, and making lobbying illegal are necessities so that we don't fall prey to corrupt politicians again," Lauren said.

"As well as passing a constitutional amendment that our federal budget must be balanced each year. It's the only way to never again go down that debt trap," Julia said.

"Julia and Deborah, you have your work cut out for you to help lead this nation into true freedom and reform. When I was praying prior to this trip, God showed me the identity of five nations in the world whom He's asked me to help Him disciple. I was really glad to hear that you all felt 'freedom' is the United States of America's identity because that's what God showed me. The enemy seems to attack the very identities of people and nations so they don't achieve their purpose and give God glory. And yet, the identity of nations can seem obvious once we think from that perspective. After God showed me the identity of my nations—of the United States, France, Italy, Israel, and Russia—I could see their identities trying to shine forth and also the opposite happening because of demonic attack and corruption," Ava said.

"Don't leave us in suspense! What're the identities of your other nations?" Jenna said.

"France's identity is *love*. They're to exhibit the love of God for humanity, the love of people for Jesus, and for people loving each other well. France, when walking fully in her identity, will have the highest rate of pure romance, healthy marriages and families, and will be known for pure worship of Jesus. France is a lover not a fighter. The attacks against France and her identity can be seen in the perversions of adultery, sexual sin, prostitution, rudeness, fatherlessness, and by being a nation not currently known for loving Jesus."

"Wow! I can totally see that," Elle said.

Ava continued, "Italy's identity is *father*. They're to show the kindness and strength of fathers in protecting, promoting, giving identity and safety to those they father. People are drawn to Italy to learn what it is to be fathered well and learn their own identity as a child of

God. We are all called to be sons and daughters of God. And Italy is a nation called to teach the world what a healthy father and family is. Unfortunately, the enemy has had a foothold there and has propagated sexual abuse by fathers, specifically through the church. Fathers are supposed to lead families and provide resources. Instead, some spiritual men have been taught, through the church, that to spiritually father someone, they cannot have a wife or children, and many have abused their spiritual children through sexual abuse. And instead of providing resources for generational legacies, there has been a stealing and a hoarding by the enemy through the church. Fortunately, God is exposing the evil and bringing restoration and restitution. Italy will walk in her God-given identity and destiny showing the earth who the heavenly Father is."

"You're right. This is fairly intuitive, but I've never thought of nations having identities before," Deborah said.

"What about Israel?" Alexa asked.

"Israel is called to *covenant*. They're to showcase what it means to walk in covenant with God. God has covenanted with Israel and with His people to be a father—to protect, to love, to promote, and to give identity to His people. God desires deep relationship with those He's in covenant with. And He wants to be in covenant with every person on the planet. Jesus died so that we could be in covenant with Father God for all eternity. All that recognize and receive Him as their Savior come into covenant with God. And Israel is where Jesus will return at the end of the age. God will always protect Israel because He promised. The enemy hates covenant and is trying to destroy God, His people, and His land. The enemy has always enraged nations against Israel and the Jewish people. It's because they're called to display God's nature, His favor, and His love to the world. One of the enemy's biggest attacks against the Jewish people is to blind their eyes that Jesus is their Messiah. He's the One they've looked for and been promised. It's been hard on God's heart that His people whom He pours out protection, favor, finances, and love receive all of His benefits, but many haven't responded with their heart. All who have eyes to see will see Jesus as Messiah."

"As you said that, I can feel Jesus's tender heart toward the Jewish people and also His heart of longing for them to know Him," Elle said.

"Yes, the atmosphere definitely changed when you talked about Israel," Jenna said.

"What about Russia?" Alexa asked.

"I almost laughed when God told me Russia's identity," Ava said. "Mostly because Russia seems anything but it's identity."

"What is it?" Jenna said.

"Russia's identity is *mother*," Ava said.

"But of course! Mother Russia!" Deborah said.

"I know. Except, she hasn't been very warm or cuddly over the years!" Ava laughed.

"That's for sure. Been a little confused about her role in the world, I'd say," Elle said.

"Yes, Russia is called to be a mother. A mother nurtures, loves, instructs, and guides. It's obvious where the enemy has inroads against the call of Russia. Government controlling and providing in a communist economic system does not empower or train people well. It's providing in a way that crushes and controls the human spirit," Ava said.

"And what about the way Russia has basically 'eaten her young' over the years through the harsh dictators who've practiced genocide? And the way that Russia, over the generations, has not allowed people to practice religion or know God?" Julia said.

"Russia has had massive spiritual attacks over her identity. I believe the war has been over whether she'll become a sheep nation or be a goat nation, like the Bible describes in Matthew 25. I'm fighting for the people of Russia to know Jesus and also the nation of Russia to be found righteous. I've read in Revelation about Russia's prophesied role in the end-times, but I've been praying that she can become a sheep nation aligned with the purposes of heaven instead. I don't want any of the nations that God has given me responsibility for to not know Him or be found faithful," Ava said.

"I can feel that the atmosphere shifted again. Now, I feel the fear of the Lord for us to be responsible for stewarding His heart and His desires here on earth," Elle said.

"That's a good way to describe it. Makes me wonder if I have nations to steward for him," Alexa said.

"I think we'll all spend time in prayer asking the same thing and what that looks like," Lauren said.

Chapter 10

❦◈❦

A few minutes before 2:00 p.m., the ladies walked down the gorgeous corridor to the entrance of the Senate Appropriations Committee room where the remaining eighteen of the thirty-one senators and their staff were preparing to meet. The ornate archways and the murals decorating every inch of the ceiling and walls made the women feel they were in a Michelangelo painting. Lauren stopped, laid her hands on the wall next to the doorway, and prayed that all who entered here would partner with the Lord with His priorities for this nation. Jenna, Alexa, and Elle joined her in declaring that the reverential awe of the Lord would guide the financial decision-making for the nation. This committee was one of the hardest hit when the arrests for treason, money laundering, and insider trading came. As the meeting came into order, Julia addressed the room.

"Thank you all for coming today. I believe this is one of our most important meetings where we will get clarity and direction for our future. I want to introduce Ava Wellington to you as well as her team of ladies. Alexa, Jenna, and Elle, please wave hello. They are here from Redding, California, to help us reset with our identity and purpose and allocation of resources, for the future after our world has seemingly turned on its head."

The senators looked on as Ava began speaking.

"Good afternoon, distinguished senators and staff. Thank you for hosting me and my team here today. We're honored and encouraged by what we believe the Lord will impart to you all. I know that as the senators who remain here in Washington after the cleansing of government leaders, or are newly elected, your hearts are to rebuild this nation. And yet you may not agree with one another on discretionary spending priorities. Therefore, I'd like to talk to you about what God has given the United States as her unique identity and purpose and also the unique identity and purpose of the Democratic and Republican parties. Everything always flows from identity and purpose. If we don't know that we have a specific purpose or identity or agree on what those are, we don't know how to move forward in unity.

"My pastor, Kris Vallotton, had a vision years ago where he saw words floating around in the air — words such as liberty, responsibility, women, children, economics, and others. The Lord arranged them in order above each other in different capacities and then spoke. The Lord said there is truth and higher truth, and there are levels and order of truth. In scenarios, you must not violate high truth to validate lesser truth. For example, the rights of women are very important. Women have the right to be free, to be healthy, to be empowered. However, when looking at the truth of women's rights regarding abortion, women's rights are a lower truth than the higher truth of a baby's right to life. The right of the autonomy of a woman's body has to be a lower priority than the right of the life of the baby she is carrying. When women's rights are valued higher than a baby's right to life, we've violated higher truth in favor of lesser truth. Therefore, we must empower women in ways that don't disempower or violate the higher truth of the rights of the unborn. A true moral society will understand and put truth in order of correct priority. From a governing standpoint, when we know that the baby's right to life is higher truth, we don't transgress that through the practice of abortion, Not to mention the higher truth of not murdering anyone, born or pre-born. Instead, we make laws and provisions to help women, regardless of how the baby's life came to be, be empowered in the bringing of that child into the world and helping both the women's and babies' needs from there. Those provisions could be through adoption, a financial safety net, relationship, vocational, and life skills training and other help. We've had our financial priorities wrong by funding abortion clinics instead of funding women's aid. Also, the children's lives are important, so priorities need to be in place to help those children once they are born.

"Another example of truth and higher truth is the truth of helping our different groups in society—groups like children, minorities, the poor, and others. Higher truth is the way in which we help needs to empower them and not crush their spirits through socialistic avenues. It's been proven throughout history, including the initial settlements at Jamestown and Yorktown, that when people are not free to own their own property and free to reap the benefits or consequences of their work, they don't produce their best. When the government, through mercy or control, provides for people economically, it can actually disempower them. Recent history in countries like Russia, Venezuela, and Cuba illustrate this point clearly. Even the more socialist European nations with high taxes and social programs have much lower innovation proportionate to more capitalistic countries. The higher truth in these instances has to be the embracing of economic principles that empower the human spirit for freedom and innovation while devising principles that aid. Scripture tells us clearly that while God loves us all equally, He does not give us equal gifts or resources. Our government should not try to achieve a goal that God isn't. We'd benefit to understand and evaluate our political proposals by looking at Scripture regarding kingdom financial principals. For example, in Luke 19:11–26, Jesus illustrates the parable of the minas which says that God gives each of us different abilities, resources, and favor and expects us to be faithful to multiply what He's given us. We're evaluated on what we each have to steward, not what anyone else has. Therefore, equality financially can't be a goal of our government.

"I'd be remiss not to mention here the deep corruption of the elite banking families who hijacked entire nations' finances through the central banking systems for their sole profit in stealing the wealth of the world and creating a one world order. There is one word for that entire plan and implementation: evil. That corrupt system is being dismantled worldwide and the wealth being removed from those who stole it. May our eyes be forever opened and that never happen again.

In the meantime, for you all going forward, you'll have to make different financial decisions for the nation. The financial weight that nations have carried because of central banks that caused inflation and the debt load created by borrowing the money printed from the federal reserve and by the corrupt overspending of government through politicians' money laundering. In addition, people were never supposed to be able to support a family on minimum wage jobs. Those are entry level positions designed for high school and college students. People are to get more training or education to move up into a higher-paying job. So the concept that we're to raise minimum wage to support a family isn't the answer. Yet one of the reasons the cost of living is so much higher than it ever has been is directly related to the effects of the central banking system. Now that, that is being removed, the overall economic impact on everyday Americans should improve in all areas including the cost of a college education. The state of our nation should cause you, as a leader, to weep, repent, and truly reform our economic system.

"As politicians, you often have to have one stance on an issue, and that's not realistic for problem solving. What is more helpful is identifying truth in order of importance. That will help you govern with wisdom regarding your agenda and available resources."

The senators were listening intently, and the staffers were taking notes.

Ava continued, "We also have to recognize that as soon as government gives aid or incentives to any group, whether it's for minorities, colleges, specific states, or corporations through tax relief, they've necessarily disfavored other groups through unfair competition and disparity of resources. Was our constitution written to bring favor to certain groups that lawmakers choose on any given day? Is that the purpose of government, or did man just decide to appropriate resources that way for personal gain? I'd propose that our Founding Fathers did not write our constitution with the goal in mind of funding pet projects or other nations for under the table personal gain. For our nation to function in a healthy manner, the higher truth is abiding by the standard our constitution set. Lower truth is helping groups through the designation of resources. We either look at specifically what our constitution legally allows and follow that, or at some point in our future, there will be a civil war similar to the Revolutionary War to achieve freedom from the tyranny of England. Each of you was given the mandate from heaven to bring God's government to earth, whether you recognize that assignment or not. To whom much is given, much is required. Each one of you will give an account to God at the end of your life for your service to this nation. I pray that you all would hear from heaven, "Well done, good and faithful, servant." Ava looked at the senators gauging their response to this admonishment.

The Lord whispered to Ava at that moment to call the senators and staff to repentance and restoration with Him.

"I know that responsibility feels heavy, but just know that the Lord gives grace to those He calls to serve Him in leadership roles on earth. I think now is a good time to set our hearts before the Lord. He just told me that some of you don't know Him, and He wants to offer you an opportunity to receive Jesus as your Savior for the forgiveness of your sins. Others of you know Him but need to align with His agenda for the world and a few of you just need to receive more of His grace for your journey."

Ava led the group in a corporate prayer of repentance and the receiving of Jesus as Savior and Lord and into alignment with grace for His mission. Nearly everyone joined in. Elle caught Ava's eye and nodded at the lightening of the atmosphere. She also saw a number of demons lose their hold on people as the people anchored to God and truth. Angels escorted the demons from the room.

While Ava was speaking, Jenna, Elle, Alexa, and Lauren were silently praying over the room and the proceedings. They could feel that the senators were not yet ready to hear about moving forward in unity. Jenna approached Ava and whispered to her that the political spirit was still too active and the revelation Ava had to impart would land on deaf ears. Ava nodded her thanks to Jenna and the ladies and asked the Lord what to do. After she heard from God, she proceeded.

"There's a demonic political spirit that has divided our nation and our leaders. A political spirit is evidenced by those influenced by it with the need to 'win' no matter what and distance themselves from those they disagree with. It is an extremely divisive, self-serving, accusatory, and condemning spirit. It doesn't allow for reason or collaboration or even the ability to discern truth. Pastor Nate Edwardson says, 'The political spirit seeks to win not serve.' I'd planned to use this time together to talk about the identity and purpose of our nation and our political parties, but without first dealing with the political spirit, I'd only waste your time and mine.

"Please take a minute to search your heart about whether you truly want to repent for partnering with a political spirit. It's your choice, but I believe it's the only way forward for this nation."

The chairman of the committee spoke up, "Our best efforts have gotten us here."

He looked around at all the senators present and said, "I don't think we have a choice but to do things God's way. If these women are discerning what is going on correctly, then I say we do what they say. Everyone agree?"

Slowly, the senators each nodded. The Chairman turned the floor back over to Ava.

"Thank you, Mr. Chairman. Please repeat after me. Father, I repent for dividing, accusing, being self-serving, and condemning and trying to win and not serve. Please forgive me. I repent for partnering with a political spirit of division instead of working for the benefit of the nation regardless which political party I'm aligned with. Please send your Holy Spirit and your angels of collaboration, strategy, unity, and provision to help us lead our nation."

At the conclusion of the prayer, a literal wind blew through the room, and many began yawning and coughing. Everyone was astonished by it. Elle spoke up to explain to everyone what was happening in the spiritual realm.

"What you just witnessed was the Holy Spirit and the angels cleansing out the demonic spirits associated with the political spirit. The spiritual realm is real and impacts the natural realm." Elle paused as she watched as angels removed the blindfolds off of the eyes of the hearts of some people in the room. "The Lord just showed me there are a few of you whom

He wants to re-extend the invitation to for repentance and salvation."

The men and women whom Elle saw have their hearts enlightened nodded their agreement. Elle led them into repentance and salvation and then deferred back to Ava.

"Have you ever wondered how in biblical times Jesus's apostles were willing to be martyred for the Gospel and how our Founding Fathers were willing to lose their lives and their fortunes to defend this nation? It's simple. They received the baptism of fire from the Holy Spirit. Purpose, clarity, hunger for God, love, resolve, and power are released with the baptism. Everyone who wants to receive the Holy Spirit baptism who has already received Jesus as their Savior, please repeat after me. Holy Spirit, I receive your baptism of fire, power, and love right now. Thank you for giving me passion, purpose, and power to serve your kingdom."

A second wind blew through the room resulting in more yawning and coughing.

"Most of you are wondering why you all are yawning and coughing right now. It's because you're being individually delivered of some demonic spirits by the Holy Spirit. I know it sounds a bit creepy, but the demonic can reside inside and come out on the breath of a person when they're delivered. You can read about it in Mark 5 in the New Testament when Jesus delivered the demonized man in the Gadarenes region. It's important after deliverance to pray for the Holy Spirit to fill and occupy the places the demons left."

Ava prayed for the Holy Spirit to fill the freshly delivered Christians. She explained to them that the Holy Spirit sovereignly delivered them into freedom and the importance of maintaining their freedom through not partnering again with a political spirit. She also told them that only Christians should be delivered because afterward, they need to be filled with the Holy Spirit, and those who aren't Christians don't have the Holy Spirit living inside of them.

"We don't have time to talk more about deliverance. I'm sure some of your theology didn't include Christians having demons, but your personal experience of just getting delivered by the Holy Spirit helped line up your theology with Scripture. I can see the peace and clarity in your minds now. If you're interested in further intentional deliverance, I'll leave some ministry information with Julia," Ava said.

"We just dealt with the political spirit, and I think we should also address the bureaucratic spirit. The bureaucratic spirit operates exactly as its name suggests. It partners with and releases spirits of confusion, frustration, control, inefficiency, and anger. It's these spirits that do not allow you to write legislation that is easily understood. It literally puts a veil of confusion over everyone it impacts.

"I know you've all wondered why even though you each are intelligent and well spoken, you can't write a bill that's easily understood. It's the bureaucratic spirit. Want to repent and get free from it?"

"Yes, Ma'am!" The Chairman said, and everyone laughed.

"Repeat after me. Father, I repent for wanting power and superiority for myself. I repent for partnering with bureaucracy, confusion, control, inefficiency, anger, and frustration. Please forgive me and deliver me from any and all of those spirits. Please fill all vacant spots in me with the Holy Spirit."

Jenna, Alexa, Elle, and Lauren moved around the room praying for people as they were delivered.

"Getting delivered from the bureaucratic spirit is not the same as having to pass a bill first to see what's in it. That's just a spirit of stupid!" Ava said.

Her unexpected humor caught the senators by surprise, and they all erupted in laughter.

"We did not get to what I thought this meeting was about. God obviously had other plans and intentions. We're going to adjourn for today, and we'll reconvene tomorrow morning at ten like previously scheduled," Ava said.

Julia thanked Ava and her team as the senators and staffers slowly filed out of the committee room.

Chapter 11

❧❖❧

"That was intense!" Elle said.

The women all agreed as they brushed themselves off from any residue from the meeting and prayed for a fresh infilling of the Holy Spirit for each of them.

As they exited the Capitol Building onto the National Mall, Deborah said, "I made dinner reservations for us at Old Ebbitt Grill. We still have a couple hours if there's anything you, ladies, want to see in the city? I, personally, love to stroll through the Botanic Gardens right here next to the Capitol. My preferred time is the *Season's Greenings* holiday show. The World of Orchids just ended, and those were gorgeous."

"I'd love to walk through the Botanic Gardens! What do you all want to do?" Ava said.

The remainder of the ladies decided to walk the city to take in the beautiful cherry blossom trees. They headed toward the Supreme Court and the Library of Congress while Deborah and Ava entered the outdoor portion of the Gardens. Deborah showed Ava her favorite "secret" garden of Bartholdi Park: a two-acre garden with private benches and a lovely water fountain.

"This is one of the best places in the city. I come here often to reflect and rest. I'm glad to have time to talk to you, Ava. I am intrigued by all that has happened today. I've read about all these things in the Bible but haven't personally seen or experienced them. I feel so much lighter inside after the meetings today. Can you please tell me more about personal deliverance?" Deborah said.

"Sure. First, let's talk about the Greek word *sozo* that Jesus used. We read the translation in the Bible as "saved," but it literally means "saved, healed, delivered." The difference is significant because what Jesus intended for us when we came to know Him was for us to know Him as Savior, be filled with the Holy Spirit, be delivered from the demonic spirits, and be healed physically and emotionally. As the church, we've not strategically ministered freedom to people all that Jesus commanded. My own experience with God took seven years to get saved, healed, and delivered. We would have a much higher success rate of making disciples if we intentionally brought freedom and intimacy with God in each of those areas immediately upon a person receiving salvation." Ava paused to examine a small flowering bush.

They ambled over to look at the flowing fountain that Deborah said was beautifully lit at night.

"I agree! Now that I've had a taste of the freedom from deliverance, I want total deliverance," Deborah said.

"My initial deliverance experience was profound because it was extensive and easy, mostly because I'd already renewed my mind to the truth of Scripture prior to the deliverance. I maintained that freedom and gradually got more freedom over the next decade. I know we're all works in progress maturing to look like Jesus, and that involves a process. However, once I began teaching ministry students, I saw the need for a faster, more complete deliverance process. I saw Christians still being harassed by the enemy with sickness, financial lack, relational problems, and other things. We were experiencing the first part of John 10:10 where the enemy comes to steal, kill, and destroy, but we weren't seeing enough of the promise of Jesus in the latter half of verse 10 where He says He came to give life and life more abundantly."

"I keep hearing the prophetic words about our world being in the beginning stages of the next spiritual Great Awakening and the billion soul harvest. I'm someone who specializes in logistics and process, and I honestly don't know how we as the body of Christ are going to disciple all the new converts," Deborah said as they moved to sit on a bench sheltered by expansive foliage.

"I too think a lot about those things. I've partnered with churches where pastors have put a process of healing, deliverance, and equipping in place so that they can meet the needs of those in their congregation and those from the harvest God will bring to them to steward. I'm sure many churches worldwide are also preparing."

"That's good to hear. I often feel, as Julia's chief of staff, that I'm the pastor of our office. In DC, we have a lot of young men and women who work very hard for our nation and have unique challenges because of the long hours and the nature of our work. I started having a private pastor come in weekly to meet with any interested staff. That has really lightened the load for the younger people in the office. Now, I see we need to incorporate deliverance to those who are saved, too."

"I love that you're doing that! That is so wise. After my own deliverance experience taking years, I researched ways for anyone to experience freedom without having to spend a lot of money or travel to a specialty ministry. Working with a team, we found a system that is comprehensive. I'll tell you the overview now, but I'll also email it to you. I know a few scriptures, including Deuteronomy 5:9–10, say that the consequences of the iniquity of the fathers will go three to four generations, but the blessing of righteousness will go a thousand generations. I observed in my students that the first and second generation Christians struggled more than Christians who had a strong family heritage until they went through generational deliverance. That seemed to level the playing field, although they still had to continue renewing their minds and often still had brokenness in their extended family relationships. I saw such transformation in all the students who prayed through generational repentance that it encouraged me for the coming harvest of souls and their transformation," Ava said.

"What is the generational repentance process? Does it take long, and is it expensive?"

"It takes fifteen to twenty hours and $50 to buy two books. A Christian can pray aloud repentance prayers and cleanse their generational line all the way back to Adam of iniquity and sin. Once sin is confessed, God remembers it no more. We know what we've individually sinned in and can confess it, but we don't know what our ancestors did that wasn't confessed and, therefore, can still impact the current generations. Generational repentance tears down the demonic high places of idols in our family lines. The books of 1 and 2 Kings in the Bible mention many times whether kings tore down or rebuilt the demonic high places. It always impacted whether the next generation rebelled or remained faithful in worship of the Lord. I've seen hundreds of people transformed and impossibilities solved doing generational work. We've seen people healed of tumors, family relationships healed, jobs gained, addictions healed, and finances restored."

"I can see why you're excited about this with all of those testimonies!" Deborah said.

"For sure. To God be the glory. Anyway, this is the process. First step, we pray aloud all the prayers from the book *Silencing the Accuser: Restoration of Your Birthright* by Jacquelin and Dan Hanselman. They paid a large cost for the revelation from God. This book takes care of the ancient sin roots. The book of Ecclesiastes says there's nothing new under the sun."

Ava continued, "Next steps include praying through freemasonry repentance. Kanaanministries.org has a good druid prayer that takes care of the ancient roots of freemasonry through repentance of druidism. The Druids were the ancient magicians illegally trafficking in the spiritual realm before Christ. Their influence continues into present day. People who are really gifted in the prophetic benefit the most from the Druid repentance prayer. Their gifting gets sharper and more accurate, probably because their ancient ancestors were Druids and were likely called to be prophets for God."

"Can you explain to me why Freemasonry is a problem? I thought it was just a professional service organization," Deborah said.

"That's a great question. Freemasonry has its initial roots in biblical times and later in Europe beginning in the Middle Ages and the early 1700s in the United States. In the entry levels of masonry, members are recruited to be part of the professional service organization. Most don't know what happens and don't progress into the higher degrees of Freemasonry. The highest levels openly declare Lucifer is god and worship him in ceremonies that mock the sacredness of Christian faith."

"Oh, that's awful! I didn't know that about freemasonry," Deborah said.

"The spiritual component affects any members and their families no matter the level or their knowledge. The masons embedded curses on members and family that leave the organization. That's why as part of the overall generational deliverance, we include Freemasonry as an important step. Almost everyone in the world has it somewhere in their background, so I recommend the repentance even if there isn't any personal knowledge of a family member in Freemasonry or its offshoots like the Elks and other clubs.

"It's personal for me because my liver failed when I was in my early thirties. My doctor at Mayo Clinic wasn't able to ascertain the cause and estimated I was six to twelve hours from death. He also said it was a miracle I lived because the mortality rate for the failure was 100 percent. Unbeknownst to me, at 2:30 a.m., the night I lay dying in bed, a friend of ours had a dream where the Lord appeared to her and said, 'It's a battle for Ava's life unto the death. Get up and get the head pastors to pray for her healing and her life.' She took the dream literally, called the pastors, and they all prayed. The next morning, I got out of bed and began the restoration process."

"Wow. That's intense. I got the full body goosebumps when you talked about the dream."

"Yes, the God-bumps. I'm so thankful for God's healing and intervention so that my babies didn't grow up without their mom. I asked God later why my liver failed. He told me I had unconfessed unknown freemasonry in my family line. Years later, during a sozo healing and deliverance appointment, the minister got a word of knowledge confirming that my liver had failed because of a link to freemasonry. Walking through that experience is the major reason I'm so passionate about everyone going through generational deliverance," Ava said.

"I can see that. I'm definitely going to follow your process for freedom for my family line. Are there any other steps?"

"Jubileeresources.org has a comprehensive freemasonry repentance prayer. However, we saw that just repenting from freemasonry wasn't setting people free fully. The Lord showed Dr. Ron Horner that there were consequences set forth by the enemy for involvement in freemasonry, so even when someone repented, they still were under the judgments. Breaking off the judgments of the enemy loosed people into freedom. Dr. Ron Horner wrote *Overcoming the False Verdicts of Freemasonry* to break off the judgments once freemasonry has been repented of. His book is our final step."

"Does every Christian have to pray through all of this?"

"No. As long as each person confesses their individual sin, one person in a generation can take care of the generational line. For example, when I prayed through the steps above, that took care of my siblings, my parents, blood aunts and uncles, grandparents, and so forth. It also took care of my half of my children's bloodline. My husband had to do the repentance work to take care of his family and our children. We saw so much liberty in our family after we prayed through all of that."

"I'm intrigued and can't wait to get to work!"

"One of my favorite testimonies is when one of my student's brother was scheduled to go to rehab for the third time. He was a Christian but had been struggling. The Lord privately asked her to do the generational work. She did the work, and a few days before her brother was to leave he told her, 'I don't know what happened, but it's like the weight of the world came off my back. Now I feel like I can succeed in taking care of my own life and getting clean.'"

"Powerful. The weight of his generations came off his back."

"Exactly. We owe it to Jesus and to our families to repent so we can walk in freedom and bring Jesus the full reward of what He paid for on the cross of Calvary."

The ladies got up from the bench to continue looking at the flowers in Bartholdi Park. They were both tired after all that had transpired during the day, so they walked silently, each left to her own thoughts.

Chapter 12

❧❖❧

A t 7:00 p.m., the group walked through the ornate marble arches into Old Ebbitt Grill. The restaurant was lively and full with congresspeople, senators, and White House officials. The central location near the White House made the restaurant a popular place to gather after a long day of work. The ladies walked past the long highly polished bar area filled with patrons to their table toward the rear of the elegant Victorian-style restaurant. Julia and Deborah waved to a few of their colleagues before sitting on the plush velvet booth seat side of the table.

"This looks like the place to see and be seen," Alexa said.

"It can be. A lot of work is continued after hours in DC restaurants," Deborah said.

"Everything looks good on the menu. What do you recommend, Julia?" Ava said.

"For starters, I'm a fan of the oysters Rockefeller, the crab and artichoke dip, and the calamari. The entree salads are all good. For main dish entrees, I especially like the jumbo lump crab cakes, the pan-seared scallops, the pan-seared Atlantic salmon, and the trout parmesan. Also, if you're interested in more traditional faire, the hamburgers are delicious."

Deborah, the ever efficient organizer, said, "Why don't we share a few of the appetizers Julia suggested and then each order our own entree?"

"Sounds great!" Lauren said.

After ordering, the ladies' discussion turned to talk of their husbands and children. Each family was unique and yet similar, and the friends were able to bond more as they understood each other's primary world of family. As they left the Grill, Julia suggested they walk to see the White House night illumination. They all enthusiastically agreed.

"I actually prefer the backside view of the White House from Lafayette Park. I enjoy seeing the comings and goings. It also reminds me of Jerusalem's Wailing Wall in that much prayer happens here," Julia said.

As Ava gazed at the People's House, she felt thankful for this great nation they were privileged to live in. She silently prayed that they'd be found faithful as a sheep nation and that they'd steward the planet well for God. She could feel the other ladies' prayers going

up to fill heaven's bowls, too, and could feel the
pleasure of God for His daughters. Before long,
they made arrangements for the morning and
then bid each other good night.

Chapter 13

＊◇＊

J ulia and Ava met up in the morning for
their walk. The city was already bustling
with purpose and with traffic. The air felt
fresh, and the cherry blossom trees provided
a stunning backdrop to the monuments. As
they passed the Washington Monument, Julia
brought up her thoughts about it.

"This monument is beautiful. It's a state-
ment piece in the city, but I can't help being
disgusted by the shape, symbolism, and by
the freemasonry connection in our nation."

"I agree. I get the creeps walking by this
but also feel the majesty of God in what our
Founding Fathers established."

"Is it possible on this side of eternity to
not have mixture in our world?" Julia wondered aloud.

"I've been talking with God about setting
our nation free from our freemasonry founding roots. I know that's on His heart too, but I
don't have the full strategy yet."

"That reminds me. I want to show you something in a back corridor at the Capitol Building before going to the appropriations' meeting room."

"That sounds slightly mysterious." Ava laughed.

Julia laughed, too, and then sped up the pace to race Ava.

Chapter 14

❦◈❦

Ava was the last of the women to arrive at Julia's Senate office. Deborah welcomed her at the door with a Starbucks mocha and breakfast sandwich.

"Aah! You're running for sainthood in my book! Thanks so much," Ava said.

"You're very welcome. I already ordered the books you told me about yesterday. And I asked my husband to do this too for our children's sake."

"You're efficient!" Ava said.

"Always." Deborah laughed.

A few minutes later, the women left the Hart Office Building on their way to the Capitol Building.

"This never gets old. I love the architecture of these gorgeous buildings," Julia said as they all processed through the Capitol security checkpoint.

"It sure is beautiful here. I was so impressed by the detail and ornateness of the

committee room and marble hallway yester-day. I tried not to gawk like a kid in there."
Ava laughed.

"Everyone does. I think if we get too accustomed to the surroundings, we can lose the reverence for our responsibility to the nation, and personal greed and entitlement set in," Deborah observed.

"Good point, Deborah. I agree," Julia said.

She expertly navigated the way through the building. She paused before opening a door to a small hallway and turned to speak with all the ladies.

"I want to show you something no one sees on the public tour," Julia said as she opened the door.

She gestured to the Capitol cornerstone on the floor and the engraved inscription that dedicated the Capitol in the freemasonry way.

"As you all know, because of the satanic roots of freemasonry, this is why it's such a problem that some of our Founding Fathers, as freemasons, allowed our nation to be falsely dedicated to Satan. It's not catastrophic. It's merely bad leaven that's woven through the government and society and allows the enemy access to this nation," Ava said.

"This is definitely something that the Lord has put on my heart to pray through here in the city. On my prayer walks, I've noticed different freemasonry dedication plaques. So far, I've seen stones like this one on the Washington and Jefferson Monuments and the mural in the House of Representatives chamber," Lauren said.

"That's interesting. What are you sensing?" Julia asked.

"I feel God wants our nation to repent from having freemasonry in our foundation and in our current history," Lauren said.

"I've felt the same thing. Intercessors across the nation have been praying into this for decades. Let's see if He shows us anything for us to do while we're here in DC," Ava said as Julia closed the door and led the way to the Senate Appropriations Committee room.

The committee members were all present, and the room was abuzz with conversation as the ladies entered. Ava and her team gathered together to pray. Ava took spiritual authority over the room, cleansed it with the blood of Jesus, commanded anything not of the Lord to leave, and asked Holy Spirit and His angels to fill the space. Elle's eyes got wide as Ava prayed, so she asked her what she saw.

Elle said, "The room feels a lot lighter since we prayed in here yesterday but as you took authority, even more shifted. Then I saw the archangels Uriel, Zerachiel, and Gabriel come in. Uriel and Zerachiel are here to stand guard and be sure God's will is done for the government and the economy. Gabriel has a scroll for you. Just hold out your hand because he's coming toward us now."

Ava did as Elle instructed and felt something light pressed into her hands.

"Gabriel wants you to eat the scroll, just like Ezekiel did," Elle said.

"Okay," Ava said.

She felt like laughing, but the solemnity of the moment restrained her. Ava, by faith, took the scroll and put it in her mouth. It tasted like honey, and her entire body flushed hot. She silently asked God to show her what the heavenly scroll contained and to give her wisdom to steward it well.

"The space is ready, and the people are ready. They'll receive what God has for them today without mocking or unbelief," Elle said.

"Amen. I just heard God say He visited all the senators in dreams last night and to ask them about it," Jenna said.

"I will. Thanks so much," Ava said.

Julia introduced Ava again to her Senate colleagues and gave her the floor.

"Good morning, Senators. I'm looking forward to a productive time together. Raise your hand if you had a significant dream last night."

The chairman raised his hand. It encouraged the other senators to do so also. Every hand in the room was raised.

"The Lord said He visited each of you last night. He showed you how much He loves you and gave you instructions for moving forward. Right?" Ava said.

Everyone nodded and was astonished not only by the night encounter with God but that everyone had one and that Ava knew about it.

"Can you sense the atmosphere is weighty with heaven's presence in here today? God sent His heavy angelic hitters," Ava said.

"Let's begin. You'll see each of you has a document in front of you compiled by Julia's office from our brainstorming the identity of the United States of America. It'll help clarify what we're talking about now.

"God gave each person on the planet a unique identity and purpose. He gives each country, state, and city individual identity and purpose. He does this because He's creative, and each entity has the opportunity to showcase a special part of Him. Just like we can't compare ourselves to anyone else, we can't compare our nation to any other. The United States of America is distinct and has a special purpose in the world. Our identity and purpose aren't hidden. In fact, if you think about it for more than two seconds, you already know what it is. The United States of America is created for freedom — freedom for ourselves and for the world. How do we understand what freedom is theoretically, and how is it practically achieved when we might disagree on the methods of freedom? I think evaluating freedom based on the concept of truth and higher truth is a valid navigation device. For example, protecting freedoms for the nation has to be a higher truth than freedom for an individual people group. If we protect freedom for the nation overall, the freedom of all citizens within the nation will be protected.

"You all have families. You understand how the choices you make in your individual life either protects or hurts your family. If you make choices to protect your family as a unit, all family members prosper. Same thought process in making decisions for your nation, just on a grander scale. These decisions need to be made independent of the political spirit because it wants to compete and win which necessitates others losing.

"As a committee, you all decide discretionary funding for our nation. One of those funding areas is for abortion. We talked yesterday about not violating the higher truth of a baby's life compared to the lesser truth of a woman's body in carrying that baby. If it were just the woman's body involved, she'd have the full right over it. Let's also look at some spiritual implications. We have the choice to partner with life regarding our words, our choices, our money. Throughout Scripture God says, 'I've set before you life and death, choose life.' Angels and demons are empowered by our words and our choices. Life choices empower God and angels to move on our behalf. Death choices literally empower the demonic spirit of death against us. When your committee chooses to fund the death of babies, you're perhaps heretofore unknowingly partnering with a spirit of death over our nation. The spirit of death doesn't just stop with abortion. It has been allowed by your empowerment to kill, steal, and destroy in our nation. We see the effects in families, in school shootings, in debt, in terrorism, downturns in the economy, in addictions, in sickness and disease."

A great sob rose up from the chairman as he fell forward on his face on the table in front of him. "I didn't know. God, I'm so sorry. Please forgive me. Please forgive us."

His true repentance caused a wave of contrition and sorrow to sweep through the room. The chairman then knelt on his knees on the floor, bowed his head, and cried out to God in tears. The other senators followed suit and got on their knees repenting before the Lord for their sins in leading the nation into death.

Ava huddled with Elle and Jenna while Alexa and Lauren continued interceding for what God was doing in the room.

"I honestly wasn't going to talk about the spirit of death released over the nation because of abortion funding today. The Holy Spirit nudged me to bring it up. I'm not sure where to go from here," Ava said to Elle and Jenna.

"I think when this lifts, God will give you the next direction," Jenna said as a wave of power came into the room.

"What's that? I felt major power just come in the room," Ava said.

Elle responded, "Yes, I just saw Michael's, the archangel, arrival. He's one tough warrior."

"Let's ask God why Michael is here now," Jenna said.

Before they could inquire of the Lord, a deeper wave of repentance hit the room. Now all the senators, staff, and Ava and her team were on the floor as the fear and awe of the Lord swept the people. Angels moved among all those on the floor touching peoples' minds to renew the neural pathways as they began to see from heaven's perspective. Other angels were touching the hearts and bringing healing to life's traumas. Demons were leaving as the repentance happened, and the lies people believed were overturned. As the angels were finishing their tasks, another wind of the Holy Spirit blew through for healing and refreshing. It was akin to pain medicine after a major surgery. This lasted for a few minutes, and then a final wave of the Holy Spirit came through. This one released power for conviction and right action to everyone in the room.

One by one, the senators sat up and returned to their seats. Despite wrinkled suits and tear-stained faces, no one seemed to notice the dishevelment.

The chairman was the first to speak. "I've never experienced anything like that before. I feel better than I have in ages. I understand now that Christianity is not mere words. Our Founding Fathers must have truly experienced God and not just heard sermons preached in their day to have done and stood for our nation the way they did."

He looked around before continuing, "Before just now, I had no idea how much I personally had compromised in leading this nation. For that, I apologize to all of you and will be publicly apologizing to my constituents and to the nation as soon as I can set up a press conference. But now, please continue, Ava. We want to hear more about the purpose and identity of our nation and political parties practically."

Ava smoothed down her own messed up hair and said, "Thank you, Mr. Chairman. We didn't expect God to show up like that, but we're very happy He did. True repentance creates humility, thankfulness, and worship. When we turn to God with worship and thankfulness, it releases us from carrying guilt and shame."

Ava took a sip of water and then continued, "Arthur Burk, of Sapphire Leadership Group, is a minister in South Carolina. He's done extensive development into government entities and individual people and cities having God-given identities and purpose. I'll share here his conclusions but encourage you to study his materials for further insight. Arthur breaks identities into seven redemptive gifts that the Lord identified through Scripture. A redemptive gift is an identity given by God to achieve a specific purpose. The United States and the Republican Party both are redemptive gift of prophet, and the Democratic Party is the redemptive gift of giver. Gift of prophet is primarily ideologically driven, specifically motivated by vision and not influenced by pain avoidance. This gift will pay any price to achieve the goal. Our founding fathers were willing to lose life and fortunes to achieve the goal of a free nation. That's a sign of redemptive gift of prophet people. Redemptive gift of prophet people and groups are strong leaders, highly adaptable, willing to sacrifice deeply, see beyond the horizon, willing to do the impossible, are problem solvers, fiercely competitive, have a strong national identity, and see the future and how it's supposed to look.

"The United States of America's strength as a prophet nation is to stay anchored on her identity as a free nation, be willing to sacrifice for herself and others, be leaders in the world, but not want to rule or conquer. Gift of prophet needs either an enemy to conquer or a significant goal to achieve.

"Another redemptive gift is a ruler whose strength is in building and intuitively putting things in place, which in weakness is drawn to nation conquering and empire building. Nations like England, Russia, and China have a ruler redemptive gift, and left unchecked, they will dominate their own people and expand their rulership over other nations. The city of Washington, DC, also has the ruler redemptive gift. The United States doesn't have that interest because she is a prophet nation not a ruler nation. There can be inherently a conflict of interests between the ruler gift and the prophet gift as evidenced by the conquering spirit in the city of Washington, DC. God ordained that the government would be located in a ruler city which carries the ability to build, ideally without a power grab. People who are drawn to live and work in DC often carry the building anointing and gifting.

"The United States' strength as a prophet nation is to identify destinies of others and see the future and how God designed it to look. She's ideologically driven and will pay any price to achieve vision; therefore, she'll stay by other nations to protect them and help them despite potential great personal cost. She'll also encourage and correct other nations.

"Weaknesses of prophet gift include never being satisfied and always wanting to make corrections, willing to defend justice and ideas at the expense of protecting relationships and love. Also, it can be driven to extremes, intensity, moodiness, judgments. When morality through the reverence of the Lord isn't there to keep a redemptive gift of prophet nation in line, greed, corruption, and power grab result. People and nations who have been oppressed can respond with violence to stop the external circumstances and control put on them despite it not being their nature. We saw this in prophet nation Germany, especially in the 1930s and 1940s.

"I think we can see how both the United States and the Republican Party fit into this gift, and yet because of all the government corruption, there's been a lack of purity, vision, and leadership. The people of the United States have been willing to sacrifice and have been abused by the leadership in the nation. Without the grounding in biblical morality and the willingness to serve for the good of the nation and not for personal gain, what we've seen is a lot of perversion. The fear of the Lord and the understanding that each politician will stand before God someday to give an account of how he/she served is the spiritual boundary that keeps politicians from falling into the ditch of greed and corruption. That and the needed natural boundaries of term limits, lobbying made illegal, and serious financial accountability regarding money laundering, campaign/foundation contributions, insider trading, and foreign financial contributions.

"Let's switch gears and talk about the Democratic Party's redemptive gift of giver. The giver is primarily concerned with stewardship and providing the resources for others to walk in their identity and destiny. Givers love to give and to solve problems through the gift of resources. Givers are intuitive, insightful, very independent, and adaptable. They tend to not be changed by others' views or persuasions.

"Three main challenges exist for givers: First, their purpose has to be stewardship, not control, selfish greed, or ambition. Second, they have to be able to accrue capital that isn't based on debt or corruption to be able to accomplish their purpose. Third, they have to give in ways that empower people, not disempower through socialistic principles that enslave people and decrease society. Because the giver is designed to hear from God about where to allocate resources, he/she needs to be strong in not bowing to man's approval. The giver is naturally strong and independent. However, without the proper fear of the Lord or without a view for empowering the generations to come, the giver can be selfish, stubborn, devoid of shame or acknowledgement of sin and personal responsibility. Also, a giver feels good by merely giving and doesn't need to solve a problem or be financially responsible to feel accomplished. This comes into direct conflict with the gift of prophet who doesn't feel good unless a problem is solved well with financial stewardship intact. How this has frequently looked up until now is that givers have spent money into large deficits and debt without the ability to steward the future generations and without a concern for efficiency or care that bureaucracy greatly mishandles money and resources. A giver has to be aware he/she is a steward, not an owner of the resources and will be judged upon the handling of the resources. Control looks like wasting resources without the conviction or intention of solving the problem because it can't give or govern with an agenda for selfish gain.

"Switzerland and Cuba are both giver nations. The expression of each is polar opposite. Switzerland has accrued enormous assets through banking, and it's a prosperous, free nation that has served the nations of the world for better or for worse, through partnering with the cabal as one of their headquarters and through nefarious uses of the vast wealth. Cuba has ascribed to Communism which has enslaved its people in its warped methodology of giving to people.

"In the US, the battle between the Republicans and Democrats has been primarily because the Republican's greatest virtue is the achievement and maintenance of freedom, and they're greatly concerned with the methodology of how the Democrats want to give and, with the Republican's foresight, don't want America enslaved like Cuba, Venezuela, and the former Soviet Union in the extreme and even the moderate enslavement of the socialist European nations like Denmark and Greece. And yet, with the severe corruption in both parties, there hasn't been financial stewardship by either party.

"Also, Republicans intuitively want the principle of freedom. Democrats intuitively want to love people. Republicans could learn from the Democrats about prioritizing people over principle. Democrats could learn the proper boundaries that lead to freedom and not bondage. Actions without purity and boundaries actually lead to abuse and not love. For example, we have to protect our nation's borders and citizens first in order to have the resources to give. We also need to have the understanding of natural and spiritual laws and that violating those leads to pain and bondage. Everything is permissible in God's kingdom, but that doesn't mean everything will come without pain and consequences. When Democrats, with the goal of love, empower socially without limits or boundaries, it actually hurts people. Feelings are important, but they make lousy leaders. There are supposed to be rules and a right/wrong way of doing things. It's okay to want rules. That's healthy. Love has boundaries.

"A father's job is to protect, provide, and give identity. We've been expecting government to father our nation instead of God fathering our nation. Because of the fatherlessness crisis in our nation, that's one reason the young in our country are attracted to socialism both economically and culturally. They're looking for government to provide for them as they've felt like orphans and haven't felt empowered. In addition, politicians from both parties have knowingly/unknowingly partnered with the deep state's nefarious agenda of death and control. Policies were made at the expense of the American people for the benefit of the few in control.

"How it's supposed to work together is this: the United States of America has the identity of freedom. Freedom for itself first with all cylinders firing for its own citizens.

Financial independence because of our own manufacturing with critical supply chain items produced in country and a balanced budget. The infrastructure of our roads and utilities healthy and up to date. Affordable trade schools and colleges so the population is educated and capable of supporting families with advanced jobs. As a model and a beacon of freedom, in order to be a light to the world, the United States of America has to protect its own freedom first in innovation, finances, strategy, protected immigration borders, and trade. Intellectual property needs to be protected and not stolen by other nations, especially China. It is imperative to abide according to the US Constitution and Bill of Rights with freedom of religion, speech, right to own property, and guns protected. From there, we can be a light to the world for freedom as a model and a resource to instruct other nations toward freedom. Freedom is an important right in the kingdom of God. It's important to Jesus that we're free to choose life or death and free to choose Him.

"The US has redemptive gift of prophet, meaning it'll lead ideologically to reproduce its identity of freedom in the world. It'll do it through modeling and through the speaking of the ideal, not through ruling other nations or compelling them to adhere to their ideas. The Republican Party has the gift of prophet so it too will want to devise ways of maintaining and bringing freedom to itself and the world. They're naturally the leaders in the US government. They see the future and how to get there. They will die on the mountain of being right and living ideologically rather than protecting relationship or teaching/training/ explaining how to get to the future they see. They depend upon the gracious nature of the Democratic Party as givers. As long as the Democrats are wise in giving, giving out of abundance and not into debt, not sacrificing the future for the now, not disempowering through socialistic principles in order to enslave or retain power for themselves, and not causing the decay of society through not having biblical moral principles in place, the parties can work together to give God His intended glory.

"Let's take a break and reconvene at 2:00 p.m. We're going to do an exercise together to practically apply what we've discussed the past couple of days," Ava said.

Everyone appreciated the segue after an intense morning.

Chapter 15

❧◆❧

"Where are we going for lunch? I'm starving," Alexa said, turning to Deborah.

"I made reservations for us on the out-door terrace of the Occidental at the Willard Washington Hotel," Deborah said.

"Sounds divine," Lauren said.

"It is. One of the best places in the city," Julia said as they exited the Capitol Building and drove to Pennsylvania Avenue.

"It's perfect weather to enjoy the patio," Jenna said as they were seated under a royal blue umbrella in the shade of the giant tree canopy.

"What a pretty hotel with the white and blue striped awnings and the stately stone building," Elle said.

"I thought the red, white, and blue donkey and elephant statues on the brick pavers at the bottom of the hotel stairs were cute," Lauren said.

"Very inclusive," Julia said.

The waiter arrived and the ladies placed their drink and food orders. Ava took Deborah's recommendation of the lobster bisque soup, the chopped salad minus the blue cheese, and an order of truffle fries to share. The ladies enjoyed the delicious food, the fresh air, and the beauty of the surroundings before heading back to the Capitol for their afternoon meeting with the senators.

Chapter 16

❧❖❧

"Good afternoon," Ava began. "Hope you all had a nice lunch and are ready for our final session. I've enjoyed our time together and feel hopeful that we've given you tools to productively move forward.

"As you're aware, the entire Congress has the impossible task of reducing US mandatory and discretionary spending over the next five years by 35 percent. It's a daunting yet necessary task. Your committee must make real, immediate cuts so that we don't incur more debt and erase the other gains.

"In addition, your job is to balance the budget within three years. The American people were so shocked by the exposed political and elite crimes; they're calling for all of your heads. If your goal is to get re-elected for anything other than serving righteously, as God is your judge, many of you won't be re-elected unless you actually fix this nation according to the Founding Fathers' design for freedom. This includes working together with all of Congress for real change, a balanced budget constitutional amendment, term limits, eliminating political lobbying, and actual justice and consequences for all."

The senators nodded at the monumental impending changes.

Ava continued, "I spent an afternoon going through the federal budget to see what you're up against and if the task is even possible. I easily trimmed $1 trillion off the top of the entire budget with only 10 percent of that coming from mandatory expenditures. You'll have to work with both branches of Congress and actually change mandatory expenditure portions for all of us and for our future generations. This is going to be painful for a lot of people, but our economy is thriving, and those laid off can be absorbed into new jobs created by the corporate sector.

"Our activity for the afternoon is to make your list and in order of your government plan to balance and reduce the budget. Remember what we talked about, and incorporate all of that in assessing what to cut.

"Here are the important items for your rubric: America's identity and purpose is freedom. If an expenditure goes against freedom, then it needs to be cut. You may need to add in more funding for things that protect freedom for American citizens such as space defense and border security. If it doesn't line up with the six areas of government listed in the constitution, it needs to be phased out and responsibility given to the states. Of the departments remaining, they need to be streamlined and efficient. Civil servant pays and benefits made commensurate to private business rates. Currently they're about 25 percent higher. Consider making pensions available at a reasonable free market rate only for those government jobs who put their lives on the line for American citizens, like the military, and law enforcement. Remember the concept of truth and higher truth in your funding values. Recall the redemptive gift of prophet for America and the Republican Party. The Republicans in your committee will have foresight into the future for America. Weigh what they see carefully regarding freedom. Consider that the Democrats in the committee see from the redemptive gift of a giving viewpoint. Weigh carefully truth and higher truth regarding expenditures. For example, we can't give out of debt but instead have to build resources and abundance to give. We can't give social love and acceptance that violates free market principles, our national security, or spiritual principles, or people will go into bondage."

She paused and then continued, "I've identified the following examples that I believe fall in line with our rubric:

1. Permanently eliminate the federal reserve and the central banking system and give responsibility to the US Treasury, thereby ending large interest payments and further debt. Put the US back on the gold standard.
2. Terminate the IRS budget and structure by implementing a flat sales tax on everything nonessential.
3. Sell the vacant federal properties, thereby terminating the annual maintenance of $25 billion.
4. End most foreign aid.
5. Restructure the military.
6. Convert health insurance by making it an à la carte system with transparent pricing.
7. Stop the ability of Congress to put earmarks in spending bills.
8. Eliminate the CIA as an agency even though not all funding for it comes from federal budget. The CIA is irreparably corrupt with its black ops budget gained through drugs and human trafficking and how they illegally got us into foreign wars and treasonous activities.

9. Remove the education department from the federal level, and give the responsibility for education to the individual states.
10. Defund planned parenthood and fund healthcare clinics for low-income women that does not include abortion. The reason clinics for women need to exist is other affordable health facilities like urgent care clinics don't address women's gynecological and breast health care.

"I'd like all of you to divide into groups of four to five senators and separate groups of four to five staffers. Please be sure there's at least one member from each political party in each group. Your task for the afternoon is to come up with a plan, which can be further modified, to balance the budget in three years and cut the overall federal budget by 35 percent in five years that correlates with our national identity and purpose of freedom.

"My team and I also want to say thank you very much for your service to this great nation. We'll be praying for you and your families. Thanks for our time together this week. We enjoyed being here with you."

Julia hugged Ava and said, "Thanks so very much for all you did with our committee and for this nation. I have a surprise for you, a desire of your heart, that I'll tell you tonight at dinner. Deborah will text you our dinner reservation details. We'll join you after our committee work here. In the meantime, have a good few hours rest with the ladies."

"Sounds great. Can't wait to hear your surprise!" Ava said.

After saying goodbye to Ava and her team, the senators and staff quickly formed groups and set to work.

Chapter 17

❧❖❧

T he ladies walked into the fresh spring DC air after the long day of meetings. After a short discussion, they decided to get iced coffees and sit outside to enjoy the weather and the city ambience. As it often did, talk turned toward their children and husbands. The conversation was interrupted by an alert to Ava's phone.

"Deborah just texted our dinner plans. Looks like the restaurant is one block north of the White House. Let's leave now so we can pray over the White House first," Ava said.

The ladies stood in the blocked off street south of Lafayette Park gazing at the majestic executive home. There was a festive feel to the atmosphere as groups of school children took pictures with their teachers and excitedly chattered about what it would be like to live in the White House. The Secret Service agents standing guard were professional and alert.

Ava asked Elle what she saw in the spirit in the compound.

Elle said, "I see watcher angels on the roof. Looks like they run the command center for the angelic hosts here. I think they alert the secret service roof snipers and control the natural protection tempo."

"That confirms what I felt was happening. I could feel the authority coming from the roof."

"The high ground is key in warfare and protection. The entire building and area appear very secure to me in the spirit," Elle said.

"I don't feel the president's spirit at the White House. I don't think he's here right now," Ava said.

"I'd agree. I don't know what the layout of the main building is but based on where I see a large group of angels, I'm pretty sure I know where the first lady is right now."

"That's probably classified information, so don't tell me." Ava laughed.

Ava all of a sudden felt the angelic hosts spring to attention and saw enormous angels streak in like missiles and land on the South Lawn of the White House. She perceived Elle watching them too. The angels were so tall the ladies could see the tops of them from the north side where they were standing. Ava noticed the secret service agent in front of them communicating on his wireless comms. Thirty seconds later, they briefly saw Marine One flying in from the direction of the National Mall before it dipped from view below the White House roofline.

"POTUS is home, just landing on the South Lawn," Ava said, and Elle agreed.

They both saw the increased alertness of angelic agents and secret service agents. The spiritual atmosphere now felt electric. The school children came to attention and responded by quietly staring at the beautiful White House.

The ladies spent another few minutes praying for the president, his family, and the nation before walking north to RARE Steakhouse & Tavern. Julia and Deborah were waiting inside the elegant restaurant. The large crystal chandelier by the expansive staircase caught Ava's eye. She enjoyed looking at everything that glitters.

"I made reservations for one of the private dining rooms, 'The Boardroom,' here," Deborah said as they were led to the regal room with blue-paneled walls.

"This room feels very stately and historical despite the newness of the restaurant," Jenna said.

"I agree. I haven't dined here yet, but it gets rave reviews. My treat tonight, and everyone has to have the Kobe beef. I hear it's exquisite," Julia said.

"Wow!" Ava squealed. "Is that the surprise? I ate Kobe beef in Tokyo years ago, and it literally was the best meal I've ever had."

"Let's hope tonight lives up to that memory," Julia said. "Actually, I'm hoping to top it by telling you that the surprise is you all have a private meeting tomorrow with the President in the Oval Office."

"What! That's so exciting!" Ava said. "How'd you put that together? That must be the desire of my heart Anna heard God talk about before we arrived."

"This is amazing!" Jenna said.

Alexa, Elle, and Lauren all agreed.

"You all know I'm personal friends with POTUS's chief of staff, and I asked him for a favor for all of you as a thank you for meeting with our Senate Appropriations Committee this week. You have a thirty-minute time slot with the president."

"That's an eternity in DC speak." Deborah laughed. "I contacted each of your husbands for your private information so that the secret service could do the proper background checks prior to your White House visit."

"Thank you both so very much. We're deeply honored and touched." Ava said.

The wait staff magically appeared then for dinner and drink orders. The evening was full of laughter, phenomenal food, and dessert.

"That was quite the reward for coming to DC. Thank you for spoiling us with Kobe beef. Definitely one of the trip highlights. I can't wait for tomorrow and can't thank you enough," Ava told Julia as the ladies all hugged goodnight.

"We'll see you at nine-thirty tomorrow morning at the White House gate on the map I gave you," Deborah said.

Chapter 18

❦

Ava and her team arrived at the White House security checkpoint at precisely 9:30 a.m. She wore her favorite red business suit. It highlighted her dark hair and green eyes. The ladies all felt the honor to walk the hallowed halls of history and were nearly giddy with excitement. Julia and Deborah joined them on the other side of the extensive security process. A secret service agent gave them visitor passes and led them to the West Wing and the famed Oval Office.

After introductions, Kris Tyndale, the president's chief of staff led them into the Oval Office. As they entered, they saw President Anderson seated behind the Resolute desk. He immediately stood to greet the ladies.

"Hello, Senator Thompson and Ms. Nelson. It's very nice to see both of you again. And you must be the Ava Wellington I keep hearing about. You and your team of ladies have really stirred up our good senators this week. I'm sure they'll come up with a wonderful budget bill I can get behind."

Ava was slightly starstruck. She knew the president was charismatic and larger than life but didn't expect him to be so approachable. The president warmly greeted each woman, and they all settled into the couches adjacent to his armchair in front of the fireplace.

The president launched right into conversation with, "So Julia tells me her nickname for you Ava is Reaganista. I'm intrigued. Tell me about it."

Ava blushed at the directness of the question. Her light skin was now tinged a rosy pink. Taking a deep breath, she said, "Reaganista is the expansion of the Reaganomics governing system of low tax rates, low business regulations, small government, and a strong national defense to further include the removal of the federal reserve central banking system. The United States Treasury under the president's direction would lead the nation with a gold backed monetary system, a balanced federal budget, no national or state debt, with freedom, and hometown values. As you know, the biggest impediment to the United States of America's identity and role of freedom for herself and the world has been financial bondage."

"Reaganista. I like that," President Anderson said.

"Mr. President, Reaganista is the inclusive term for what you're already putting in place. I know you see the big picture, and you've been putting the pieces in motion for years. I want to thank you for all you've done and for how much you love this country."

"Well, I care very much for this nation that our children and grandchildren inherit. As you know, where we go one, we go all."

The president continued, "I know the evil of a few behind the scenes over the centuries is what led us here, but can you please give me insight into the spiritual forces behind this? It occurs to me that perhaps all of the steps I'm implementing could be undone in future administrations."

"That's a very good question. Forgive me if this turns into a sermon, but I'll do my best to give you the spiritual overview of recent history," Ava said.

"As you may know, God has two primary goals for this world: reconcile people into right relationship with Him for those who choose to accept His Son Jesus's payment for sin and disciple nations into righteousness through His children. His goal is to bring heaven to earth and make earth look like heaven. Our main enemy—Lucifer, the fallen worship angel— has the opposing goals of preventing humans from reconciling with God, hurting humanity and God's heart through hurting of humanity, and turning earth into hell on earth. He operates through partnership with humans to bring about his goals.

"I believe the primary modern-day strategic plan the enemy has been working toward, and what you've spent your presidency dismantling, initially began with the Act of 1871 which secretly and treasonously made the United States a corporation indebted to the Rothschild's bank in London. The enemy enlisted further help in 1877 by giving a demonic vision to Cecil B. Rhodes on the day he was inducted into freemasonry. He had a supernatural vision of a one world order in government, economics, and religion under the rule of the British Empire. Rhodes presented his plan and partnered with wealthy families, specifically the Rothschilds and the Rockefellers. They each agreed to channel their lives and generations to build fortunes to control the world through the implementation of a central banking system and put their chosen people into positions of power. They formed an organization which still exists today called 'the Council on Foreign Relations' to educate and position members in key political and economic roles worldwide. They recognized they needed supernatural help and participated in freemasonry, in the occult, and many openly worship Satan. The government organizations formed through their secret memberships include our Central Intelligence Agency, the World Health Organization, the United Nations, and the worldwide central banking system. This insidious plan led to worldwide drug and human trafficking, world wars for the benefit of the elite banking families, pedophilia, satanic child sacrifice, the globalization of poverty, and attempted population control and reduction," Ava said.

"I think you're intelligent and intuitive to know the natural steps to take regarding the people responsible for all of this, including: arrests, seizing of assets, removing from positions of power especially in the Senior Executive Service, and dismantling organizations. Then there are the changing of government laws in areas of term limits, financial accountability checkups of elected and hired government workers and their families, making political lobbying illegal especially by foreign governments and companies, removal of the central banking system, and the backing of our currency by gold. Then the critical piece is of educating our population through the rewriting of textbooks and curriculum. As you know, cultural Marxism has gained a stronghold among our young adults."

The president nodded in agreement and asked, "Will removing the influence of these world leaders and charging them with their crimes against humanity fully fix the problem? Or is that just pulling the tops of weeds without pulling out the root?"

"There are definite spiritual steps you need to take. What you're overseeing is the birth of a new nation and a new world. We've truly entered into a new era where nothing will look the same again."

"My entire body got goose bumps when you talked about the birth of a new nation and a new world."

Ava said, "I did too, Mr. President. That was the Holy Spirit confirming what He's doing. I also see Uriel the Archangel standing next to you right now. He's going to help you with all that you need to do."

"Is he standing to my left?" POTUS asked.

"Yes, Mr. President."

"I can feel him. I wondered who that was honestly. He's with me a lot. Do I sound crazy?" The president laughed.

"No more than I do for telling you what I saw in the spirit." Ava and all the ladies laughed.

"Actually, my wife and I both feel something dark that follows us around. We've been embarrassed to say anything to anyone."

"Aah. I'm glad you brought that up. I've felt that dark presence since we came into the Oval Office. I asked the Lord what it was, and He said it's the spirit of freemasonry. It has been allowed to be here because this nation, in addition to being dedicated to God, was also falsely dedicated by some to Lucifer through freemasonry."

"That explains a lot. That's always bothered me about some of our nation's leaders historically and in current day being connected to freemasonry. I have been asked to join multiple times in my business career and always got the creeps about it."

"Wise, Mr. President."

"I don't suppose there's anything we can do about it?"

"Oh, quite the contrary. As the chief executive in our nation, there's a lot you can do about it. I had a dream a few years ago where you as president said, 'Jesus Christ is Lord over the United States.' You also declared you were putting things in place so that the people in the three branches of government would serve Jesus."

"I did say that aloud with my wife a few months after my inauguration."

"That's when I had the dream," Ava said and continued, "As far as freemasonry over this nation, you and other government leaders can repent for that fraudulent foundation. That will truly help us with the birth of a new nation and a new world."

"I got the full body goose bumps again."

"I did too. The Lord is confirming His word and His will," Ava said.

"Alright, that's what I want to do then. How do we do this?" the president said.

"Freedom starts with repentance." God is a just God. That means that because of the sin of freemasonry in our nation, our nation deserves judgment. However, He sent His Son Jesus to pay for the price of sin for all those who repent, including nations, so that He may extend mercy, grace, and forgiveness to us."

"Go on."

"Before we can repent on behalf of our nation, we also have to repent on behalf of ourselves and our generational line of anyone involved in freemasonry or any of its offshoots like the Elks, the Rainbow Girls, and others. Almost everyone in the world has freemasonry in their generational background because it was so prevalent in Europe and everywhere the British Empire extended."

"What does the repentance look like?"

"In my experience, it's an extensive repentance prayer and prayers overturning the false verdicts or consequences of freemasonry off of the family line. Ideally, on behalf of our nation, you as the president, the vice president, the Speaker of the House, the House minority party whip, the Senate majority and minority leaders, and the Supreme Court chief justice should all do the freemasonry generational repentance work. You will each get a lot of personal and family breakthrough in so doing."

Deborah, who had been listening intently, spoke up from her position at the end of the couch. "My office received a box of the books today. I'd be happy to share them with you for this purpose."

"Thank you, Deborah, that would certainly expedite this process," POTUS said. "Once the repentance work is done, then what?"

"Then you repent on behalf of the nation together," Ava said.

"I'm assuming if I corral all the leaders today and we get the work done that you would be willing to help us with that part too, Ava?"

"Absolutely, Mr. President."

The president nodded to Kris, his chief of staff, who immediately began to coordinate the details and contact the important parties.

A few pictures were taken with President Anderson, goodbyes were exchanged, and then the ladies were ushered out of the Oval Office. Julia and Deborah went back to the Hart Senate Office Building to work while Ava and her team set about on their way for the day.

Chapter 19

✥

"That meeting was a dream come true, not only for us but for God and the world," Ava said.

"I saw the cloud of witnesses peering from heaven to watch. They're so excited for what comes next for God's kingdom and the world as a result of the president's willingness to cooperate with the spiritual realm," Elle said.

"He certainly is very spiritual. Sometimes not growing up in church is helpful in not putting God in a box," Jenna said.

"I agree but am glad church carries true spirituality now," Elle said.

Ava asked, "Lauren and Alexa, what do you ladies think we need to do to prepare to take the president and the other leaders through the freemasonry repentance. I'm assuming it'll be tomorrow."

As they talked, they'd walked and were now approaching the Washington Monument on the National Mall.

"Let's sit on this circular half wall and pray about our next step," Lauren said.

"Good idea," Ava said.

After praying, the ladies came up with the strategy to pray and take communion outside the White House, the Capitol Building, the Supreme Court, and the Washington Monument. They decided to also pray over the Jefferson Monument because they knew it had a freemasonry dedication to it.

"I heard God say to start with the White House and end with the Washington Monument," Jenna said.

"Sounds like we're going to get our exercise today," Alexa said.

"And after taking communion five times, we won't need lunch either," Jenna said, and they all laughed.

The ladies headed back to the White House to pray. Fortunately, Lauren had communion supplies in her purse for such a time as this.

At the end of their prayer assignment, the ladies finished taking communion at the Washington Monument.

"This may sound cliché but I just heard the Lord say to walk around the monument seven times," Jenna said.

"Okay, we'll do that, but if it falls down like the walls of Jericho, the Lord is responsible," Ava said half-jokingly.

The ladies began to walk, silently praying as they did. As they completed the seventh time around the Washington Monument, they heard a loud crack. It startled them and all the tourists in the area. The park security responded quickly by ushering everyone out of the area and calling for temporary security boundaries around the large monument.

From a safe distance Ava said, "Well, that's very interesting. No matter what happens from here, that's confirmation that the Lord is ripping out the demonic root of freemasonry from our nation."

"I agree. It's long overdue," Elle said. "When we first approached the Washington Monument, I saw a huge black gargoyle-type demonic power sitting at the very top. It was taunting us. When we began to take communion and then walk around the monument, it got uneasy and started shifting around. As we completed the walk, that demonic power fell to the ground dead. That was the large sound we all heard. It broke the spiritual sound barrier into the natural realm. Two large angels came and swept up the body and flew off with it."

"Thanks, Elle. That explains a lot," Ava said. "It's nice to see the chips fly in response to our prayer efforts."

"I'm having so much fun!" Lauren said. "While we wait for the president to get back to us, I'd love to invite you all over to my home in Vienna for dinner tonight. My husband makes a mean lobster tail."

"Lobster is my favorite, and I'd love to see your home, Lauren. Thanks for the wonderful invitation," Ava said.

Alexa, Jenna, and Elle all agreed.

"I already invited Julia and Deborah. Why don't you ladies go back to your hotel to rest and change. I'll give you my address, and you can take the metro to my house this evening," Lauren said.

"A nap sounds divine right now," Ava said.

Chapter 20

A few hours later, Lauren picked Ava, Jenna, Elle, and Alexa up at the Vienna metro stop and drove them to her lovely home. It was a large, light-colored brick house in an established neighborhood. They entered the kitchen to see Lauren's husband, Christopher, prepping one pound lobster tails on the granite countertop. Lauren introduced the ladies to Christopher. He quickly shooed them out of the kitchen, so Lauren led them onto the enclosed porch where Julia and Deborah were already lounging. Lauren poured drinks from the pitchers of lavender lemonade and jasmine iced tea.

Ava shared the details of the afternoon prayer walk with Julia and Deborah. They all discussed their thoughts on the state of the nation. Just then Julia got a text from Kris, the president's chief of staff. He informed her that the president had sequestered all the leaders in separate rooms in the White House until they each finished praying aloud all the free-masonry repentance prayers. He said they were a go for tomorrow at 1:00 p.m. in the Oval Office.

"I'm so happy that he's taking this mission seriously," Ava said. "But I find the thought of all of them in the White House right now really funny. This is probably a first in this nation."

"Kris said the president didn't trust them to finish the prayers on their own, so he sent the Secret Service to pick them up." Julia said laughing.

"We definitely have the better evening tonight," Elle said, giggling.

"Lobster, salad, corn on the cob, lavender lemonade, jasmine iced tea, ice cream," Lauren said.

"That's because we've all spent hours already doing our own repentance work. Now it's their turn to work and our turn to play," Julia said.

"I promise I'll get mine done this week. But for tonight, I feast and play too," Deborah said.

"Deal," Julia said.

The evening was relaxing and fun. The conversation was light after such an intense week.

Chapter 21

❧◈❧

A va woke early on her last full day in Washington, DC. She could feel the atmosphere of the city was charged with electric energy and anticipation. She went for a walk alone to commune with God and process the week. As she talked with God, He reminded her of His promise in Scripture to bless nations whose God is the Lord in Psalm 33:12 and also the promise to bless those who bless Israel and to curse those who curse Israel in Numbers 24:9. The Lord instructed Ava to talk to the president about those two things and to establish the position of the United States of America on His foundation.

At precisely 1:00 p.m., Julia, Deborah, Ava, Jenna, Elle, Alexa, and Lauren walked into the Oval Office. Already assembled were the president, vice president, the newly appointed and confirmed chief justice of the Supreme Court, Senate majority and minority leaders, Speaker of the House and House minority whip, and assorted chiefs of staff.

After all the introductions, President Anderson said, "Good afternoon, Ava. Full house in here today. I was going to have this meeting in the East Room, but I had a dream last night we were all in here. In the dream, the Lord spoke to me that if we as a nation bless Israel, He'll bless us. I'd like to make that proclamation today that the United States of America stands with Israel. I've already instructed my staff that we're going to work with Israel to finish all the Middle East peace agreements."

"That's wonderful news, Mr. President. The Lord spoke that very thing to me on my walk this morning. He also told me to tell you that your intention to declare that Jesus Christ is the Lord of the United States will bring tremendous blessing to this nation because of His promise in Psalm 33:12 which says, 'Blessed is the nation whose God is the Lord, the people He has chosen as His own inheritance.'"

"I'm happy to hear that. Before we begin, I want Chief Justice Brooks to briefly tell you what happened to him last night."

Justice Brooks said, "To be honest, when the president asked us here to renounce freemasonry, I thought it was ridiculous and inconsequential to me. When I was given the book of repentance prayers, an individual space in the White House, and basically a Secret Service guard to be sure I complied, I thought I'd just do it to get it over with. I read through the first prayer aloud by rote. I have to admit the things I read began to bother me. My family has always been involved in free-masonry. I thought it was a business organization that afforded us networking favor. I learned things about this secret society that were blatantly evil. Even though I was disturbed, I still didn't believe it related to me at all because we were only in the first level."

He cleared his throat as if embarrassed to share his next thought, "Suddenly, something appeared before me that looked like a movie screen suspended in the air. I began to watch what seemed to be a strategy room. I saw what I can only describe as a very evil man/creature discussing with his minions his plan to use the Luciferian freemason organization as his primary tool to destroy the world. They had a list of family names they planned to corrupt and put in world leadership positions to enact their evil plan. The screen in front of me zoomed in on the list of names."

The chief justice paused, blinked back tears, and then continued his story, "I saw the Brooks family name including my grandfather, my father, myself, and both of my sons. I can't tell you the sorrow I felt at that point. And I felt outraged that I and my family had been so deceived to cooperate with evil. As I was processing this, the screen changed. I saw such love, such goodness. I saw God on His throne in heaven. Jesus and who I understood to be the Holy Spirit were with Him. They were holding up a baby and an enormous book. God said, 'This baby will face an immense battle, will overcome, and with others will bring peace to the planet.' They were so pleased by this child, his future accomplishments, and the heavenly reward they would give him. They turned to the book. I watched as they recorded the child's accomplishments. Unexpectedly, I saw the child's name in the book and was shocked to see it was mine. God nodded at me that this child was indeed me. At that point, I fell to my face in deep sorrow for how I have sinned against this great and merciful God. I don't know how long I lay there painfully aware of and repenting for every sin I could remember. Suddenly, I understood my need for the payment of Jesus for sin, and I received His gracious gift of salvation. I know I have a lot to learn, but I fully intend with the rest of my life to love God, serve Him, and accomplish all He wrote in His book about me."

"That's amazing! Praise God!" Ava said.

"That encounter went into the early hours of the morning. When I got up off the floor, I officially tendered my resignation from the freemasonry organization effective immediately and started the freemasonry repentance prayers over from the beginning. When I finished, I went home and talked to my wife about what the Lord showed me. She's thrilled because she has prayed for me for years. When I leave here this afternoon, we're meeting with our sons and their wives to discuss our new family legacy."

The chief justice was beaming at his newfound relationship with God.

"Thanks for sharing your story with us. I appreciate your vulnerability and candor," President Anderson said. The rest assembled in the Oval Office had all previously received Jesus as their Lord and Savior. The mass arrests and exposure of evil the previous year had shocked most of the country into searching for God and truth.

"Ava, where do we go from here?" POTUS asked.

"All of you here represent the natural leadership of the United States government. As a result, you have spiritual authority on behalf of this nation to break agreements with freemasonry and evil and declare this truly is one nation under God." Ava looked at Jenna.

Jenna nodded her agreement that everyone was ready to proceed.

Ava said, "Would you all please stand. Chiefs of staff, please hold the Bible in front of your boss. Government leaders, please put your left hand on the Bible, raise your right hand, and repeat after me. You'll say your own full name at the beginning, and when it's appropriate, say which branch of government you're the leader of."

Everyone was standing at attention. A holy hush came over the room.

When she was sure that all of heaven and earth was ready, Ava began, "I (she paused as they each said their full name) do solemnly repent for the sin of freemasonry in the founding and governing of the United States of America. I repent as the leader on behalf of the (executive, judicial, legislative) branch for freemasonry. I declare that freemasonry has no part in this nation from here forward. I declare that all evil effects, false verdicts, and evil forces connected to freemasonry must leave the United States of America now. I declare that Jesus Christ is Lord over the United States of America. I declare that Jesus Christ is Lord over the White House and the executive branch. I declare that Jesus Christ is Lord over the Supreme Court and the judicial branch. I declare that Jesus Christ is Lord over the Senate and the House and the legislative branch. I declare Psalm 33:12, 'Blessed is the United States of America whose God is the Lord, the people He has chosen as His own inheritance.' I declare the United States of America blesses Israel and the Jewish people. I declare Numbers 24:9, 'Blessed is the United

States of America who blesses Israel and the Jewish people.'"

There was complete silence in the room for a full minute as they each pondered the divinely appointed kairos moment. Suddenly, many Secret Service agents rushed into the Oval Office.

The lead agent urgently said, "Mr. President, we need to get you to safety. We're under attack. The Washington Monument just collapsed."

POTUS asked, "Is that all that's happening in DC?"

Confused by the president's question and lack of alarm, the agent radioed the command center for clarification. The response quickly came back that nothing else seemed amiss in the nation's capital.

The president looked at Ava for guidance. "You're the spiritual expert here. What's your assessment?"

Ava said, "I believe in response to all of your repentance and declarations, the evil root of freemasonry and the curse over this nation was destroyed. The Washington Monument epitomized the evil and, therefore, couldn't stand. I suspect that if you send people to examine the freemasonry stone on the Jefferson Memorial, in the Capitol Building, the mural in the House of Representatives, and anywhere else it existed, that those will also have been obliterated as a natural confirmation of our spiritual deliverance."

The president nodded to the lead agent who radioed instructions to investigate those places in the city. Everyone in the room remained silent. The awe and reverence for the Lord was tangible. Within a few minutes, confirmation of those exact things came back along with the supernatural report that there was no debris or even dust left at the location where the Washington Monument stood minutes before. Save the concrete pad, it was as if it had never existed.

The president and everyone in the Oval Office ran outside to look over the South Lawn to an empty visage. The monument was indeed gone. The Jefferson Monument could be clearly seen in the distance.

"Well, I honestly didn't expect that to happen, Mr. President. All signs of the Illuminati are now gone from the United States. Good thing you changed the American currency this year, or our entire money supply may have vanished into thin air." Ava laughed, and the president joined in heartily.

President Anderson turned to Kris and asked him to work with the press secretary to schedule a briefing to release the truth of what happened today with the Washington Monument to the American public. He also instructed him to draft an executive order to declare that freemasonry would be considered a terrorist organization in America.

"I love to build, so I'm excited to design the replacement monument that will honor the United States and honor the Lord. Think the Lord will supernaturally give us money for the project since He was responsible for the removal of the previous monument?" POTUS said and winked at Ava.

Chapter 22

≫◈≪

For their final night in Washington, DC, the ladies dined again at Old Ebbitt Grill. It was a lively affair with everyone reliving their astonishment at hearing the Washington Monument had collapsed into thin air. Alexa surmised she expected they'd all be arrested or that the president would be angry with them. They were all sure God told the cloud of witnesses to peer over heaven's balcony as He performed His supernatural surprise. Jenna laughed and said God probably took a picture of each of their expressions for posterity and His heavenly scrapbook. Elle agreed that future generations would watch the video of that moment upon their arrival in heaven. All in all, they were each thankful for what God had accomplished for America and that they got to partner with Him in another fun adventure. They couldn't wait for what He had in store for them next.

Bibliography

Burk, Arthur. *Redemptive Gifts*. Sapphire Leadership Group. theslg.com.

DeSilva, Dawna. dawnadesilva.com

Enlow, Johnny. www.restore7.org.

Hanselman, Dan and Jacquelin Hanselman. *Silencing the Accuser: Restoration of Your Birthright-Third Edition.*

Horner, Ron. *Overcoming the False Verdicts of Freemasonry.*

Howard-Browne, Rodney and Paul L. Williams. *The Killing of Uncle Sam: The Demise of the United States of America.*

Johnson, Bill Ministries. Bjm.org.

Jubilee Resources International. jubileeresources.org

Kanaan Ministries: Preparing the Bride. kanaanministries.org

Vallotton, Kris. kvministries.com.

About the Author

❧❧❧

Annie Blouin is passionate about the Lord and politics. She has keen insight into implementing God's solutions into the political realm and has equipped people how to be naturally supernatural with a sound biblical foundation for over a decade. Her heart is to see reformers influence every area of society with love and wisdom. Annie is also the author of *Reaganista's* prequel *Everlasting Doors: When the Supernatural Penetrates American Politics*, *Everlasting Prophetic: Bridging Heaven to Earth*, and *Prophetic Revelation: Keys to Spiritual Maturity*. Check out AnnieBlouin.com for more information on Annie and her teachings.

Annie has been happily married to Joe for twenty-six years, and they have three adult children, a son-in-law, and a new granddaughter who all love the Lord.

CPSIA information can be obtained
at www.ICGtesting.com
Printed in the USA
LVHW021327260422
717239LV00013B/985

9 781638 149101